CELEBRATE MYSELF

CELEBRATE MYSELF

by

JAMES BUCKLEY

Author's Note

This novel is best enjoyed with the musical accompaniment of:

Rachel Goswell's "Waves are Universal"

Mark Gardener's "These Beautiful Ghosts"

"Songs to Sing in A&E" by Televise.

Better artists by far.

*Cheers to anyone who encouraged me in this endeavour
and the American ladies' book club for their interest, none of whom
are in any way role models for Simone, (honest!) This novel would
never have seen the light of day without enormous patience and
support from my wife, Amy Buckley.*

www.myspace.com/celebratejames

For Amy and Ciaran.
Whom I celebrate every day.

Chapter One

Simone Sanders

They're dead. Both of them. It was kill them or get kicked out on my ass. So in the end what kind of choice did I have? Believe me, I argued my case. Tried to make the authorities here accept my needs, to show leniency, but they wouldn't.

"The situation has been made abundantly clear to you, Miss Sanders. You know the consequences if you continue to ignore our warnings."

I made the officious asshole stand on my doorstep when he told me this last Tuesday. It was raining so hard water was bouncing off the cheap plastic awning above my doorstep and landing on his moustache as he spoke. Didn't shake him though. Terrier-like these Brits when you give them a bit of authority.

"Our rules are there to protect everyone's best interests, Miss Sanders. There are no exceptions. You're an intelligent young woman; I don't expect to discuss this matter with you again."

Intelligent young woman? At school, I was the girl who vetted who could sit on the most popular table; at Stanford I graduated Phi Beta Kappa; I was the youngest female vice-president at the brokerage. While my female acquaintances, (I don't have girlfriends), were reading *The Rules* or *The Celestine Prophecy*, I was devouring *Liars Poker* and *Play Like a Man, Win Like a Woman*. I drank beer with the boys and bitch-slapped the women, metaphorically of course, well most of the time. This place is lucky to have me. Tell that to these small-minded bureaucrats though. Assholes would flunk me in a heartbeat.

I arrived here last month, England in the fall. So quaint, I felt excited. It was to be a fresh start after all the shit I had to put up with in San Francisco. At first it was fun, the workload was heavy but I was used to that. From the start there were a few people who didn't like me. Little tell-tale signs. They'd sit two seats away from me and then in the next class they'd be all up close and personal with someone else. But I decided it wouldn't affect me. I was here to get my MBA, have a little fun, then go back to the States and cash in. As I expected I've had to break some balls in my study group. The first meeting was tense but I remembered all the advice

1

I'd had from people who'd done this kinda shit before. Basically take a few moments to size up the opposition then hit them hard and take no prisoners.

"Simone, we've all got a valid contribution to make. We need parity of esteem here in order to realise our potential as a group."

Just listen to this stuck-up Brit, Hilary Jenkins-Spires. A real hard-ass bitch from the start. Gotta give her credit for laying down her marker from day one. Needs to be stared down though.

"So just to clarify your position, Hilary, you're proposing that we all have equal air-time, even those of us who barely speak English?"

"That appears to be the most equitable approach to me, Simone. Anyway, everyone here speaks excellent English."

Couple of eyebrows raised at this comment.

"Yeah, well life ain't always equitable, Hilary; neither is business school. We need our biggest hitters at the plate. That means me, and OK, seeing as I'm a committed team player, you too."

She half-heartedly continued to insist we should all present for an equal time, but we knew this was a good deal on the table for both of us. Before coming here I made my living in equity sales, where you eat what you kill, blowing smoke up the ass of hedge fund managers who act like they're God's greatest creation. You can't seriously tell me you can compare that to what the rest of these clowns bring to the table: mindless enthusiasm coupled with no sense of their own inadequacy. Talk the talk but piss their pants at a second stage McKinsey call-back.

"Guys, don't think for one second I don't have your best interests at heart, I lead with a tough mind and a big heart. That's why I want to put myself on the line for you here."

Look around the table here. Focus in on one particularly sorry looking specimen, little weird looking dude, think he's from Mongolia or somewhere like that. Only speaks when spoken to.

"Balbeck, I value your input here. If you've got an issue with what I'm proposing, share it with us all please."

He looks spooked and shakes his head. In the face of this display of selfless team-spiritedness, Ms Jenkins-Spires was forced to swallow hard, back down and allow us to host the presentation jointly. I decided to outflank her a little, be magnanimous, and suggested Olaf from Finland take five minutes of what just happened to be the most boring crap, explaining the statistical significance of our conclusions. Sometimes you've got to throw the little people something, I mean it keeps you popular, right? Plus the guy's English is OK, and shit is he ever built. I know the others appreciated my generosity, especially Olaf. Maybe I'll cash in on that later in term, after all a girl has needs. Of course, in the end Hilary couldn't present for shit, but hey what do you expect from someone with a name like that?

I wasn't surprised the dumb English bitch let me down; my expectations are always high. What's disappointing is other people not meeting them: family, friends, workmates, classmates, partners. My parents are a particular let-down: they just don't get how significant my achievements are. I was a latchkey kid. My father owned a hardware store in Tipton, Iowa, then Walmart opened and good as cleaned him out. To this day he's never understood it, still stays open steadily losing money, believing he's hanging on to his status in the community. Working himself into the ground running a loss-making business just to be in the local rotary club, even continues to vote Republican. Still kids himself about the loyalty of his customers, even when they walk into the store with their chain store carrier bags, making their little top-up purchases, or more likely asking for something he hasn't got and being sent to Target in Iowa City. Makes excuses for them, how what with the economy being so subdued and all that they have to watch every dime. My mother just wanted to stay at home and bake cookies, but my father's shitty business-sense forced her to work first in the store to cut down on the wage bill, then part-time as a receptionist at the local vet's surgery. It's hard-wired into my brain how she'd got the job there, the embarrassment of it. Bunter, our pet dog, (just a mutt, my parents couldn't afford a pedigree), got hit by a car. They weren't insured of course and the vet's bills, well, even in Tipton they were gonna put a hole in their already sketchy finances. So the vet took dear petrified mother aside, in front of a waiting room full of people, and said he'd operate on Bunter, they'd sort something out later. The only sound in the waiting room when he was telling her this was silence. No way were these good folks missing out on the latest instalment of humiliation for the Sanders' family. Bunter died anyway and Mom's still working there, twelve years later. Last time I saw her she was dropping me off at the airport to catch a flight here. She was squeezing my hand so hard it was hurting. Then she shoved a package in my hand. Something small, hard and flat.

"Please, Simone, take this to remind you of home. Promise me you'll take care of yourself, that you won't drive yourself too hard, let things get on top of you. You know how much your father and I worry about you."

She's clutching my hand with both hands so tightly her veins are coiled like blue rope under the surface of her aging skin. Take a look at her, you'd think she's too frail to lift a pitchbook, but there's a fierce strength in her grip today.

"Mom, I'm going to England, not another planet. Look they're calling my flight. I gotta go. You always worry too much. Anyway it's not that different to home."

Forget the shit I tell her, things here better be very different to home. I'd already worked out what I needed to do; concentrate on some serious networking, focusing on the handful of people who might actually achieve something with their lives. Make sure I stay outta trouble too, don't want to screw things up before I return to the States. Already put a few feelers out on that front, well it's never too early. All told, things have been pretty cool here. Who'd have thought it a year ago after all that happened in San Francisco.

Which is why I decided to kill these two a week ago. That afternoon, when the guy turned up on my doorstep making it clear the authorities weren't fooling around. For weeks I'd pleaded, even tried bribery, subtly at first, then more obviously, but it was no good. Goddam British are so uptight! I knew then I had to act, couldn't afford to flunk out here. No way am I going back to smiling and dialling to overpaid, undersexed assholes. Of course I could have tried to move but there was nowhere suitable, it's just too much hassle, everything over here is so damn bureaucratic. Nope, I'm staying here and I'll do whatever I have to do to make that happen.

Once I'd decided to kill them it was just a question of how? I thought of poisoning but they are picky eaters. Not surprising, the food over here sucks. Shoot them? Too difficult to get a gun in this goddamn country. No wonder the crime figures are so high. Anyway, needed a solution, ironically came to me after yet another phone call from my Mom, this time rambling on about her work. Something about the nice new drug rep who had called in last week and was asking after me, turned out we'd been to school together. Was making my lack of interest clear to get her off the damn phone when it struck me, minimum risk of getting caught and sure to do the job. All it required was a call to my dealer, asking for something a little different this time, premium price offered of course, and I'll take a little of the usual. Shouldn't really as I barely touch it, but this is all very stressful as I'm sure you can appreciate. Next, venue and timing. Wednesday late afternoon was ideal, a popular study group time and less people around as it's apparently sports afternoon. Like I care. Informed my study group that we'd be meeting then, I might be a little late, but expected them to be there. After killing them I'd dispose of their bodies in the river.

By ten past four, they're dead. I came up behind them in the sitting room of my one bedroom flat and injected them with a shit-kicking dose of ketamine. Wasn't easy. Thought I'd found the perfect needle, but plunging it through the gristle and bone at the back of their neck was damn difficult. The first one was quicker 'cause he was still fast asleep. But the second started stirring soon as I climbed astride him. Tried to pin him to the floor between my thighs but he was strong. Didn't help that I was still in high heels. He whimpered a bit after I punched the needle through his skin. Just stroked his head softly and told him to go back to sleep. I loved my babies, really I did, but when they told me I couldn't keep my Dobermans here with me in my university flat, I couldn't bear to let anyone else have them. You see, no-one else could have looked after them properly. Sometimes you know, you just have to make the hard decisions in life. Anyway, I should parcel the bodies up and get rid of them. Gonna need a bit of help. Not some eurotrash playboy with a two seater sports car either. I need a dumbass with a strong arm, a car with a trunk and a lack of curiosity. Better get into gear, don't want to keep my study group waiting too long. Can't give Hilary any excuse to challenge my position. Anyone would think this place was Harvard!

Harry Stanton

"You see, Marianna, the capital asset pricing model is all about the relationship between risk and return. Just think of it this way; your boyfriend is the risk free rate, OK? The average, friendly, platonic, let's-go-have-coffee-relationship you have with the guys on the course, that's the market rate, yeah?"

She squints her big brown eyes and bites her bottom lip, but I think she's getting it.

"OK, now stay with me here. Let's say our relationship is the beta. Right now I'm just one of those 'Hi, how-are-you-guys', but what if we were to start to have an affair? Then I become more than just the normal bloke you hang out with. Sure the risk to your relationship with your boyfriend would increase, but so would the return you get in terms of the fun you'd have with me. In other words Marianna, let's get naked and raise the beta!"

"Stop it, Harry! All you ever think about is sex, you know I'm not going to sleep with you. Don't you ever take anything seriously?"

Despite trying to appear offended, she's struggling not to start giggling.

5

"Marianna babe, the Capital Asset Pricing model's a load of crap, you'll never need to know it again after January's exam. Just practice solving the equation until it's second nature then forget about it."

"Yes, but Harry, I want to work in finance afterwards, don't I need to know this stuff? Ulrich says…"

"Fuck what Ulrich says. He's never worked outside a University classroom in his life. Listen, Marianna, you're hot…."

"Stop it!"

"Why? It's true, you're a babe and you've got personality. Babes with personality get jobs, and it won't be down to your knowledge of modern portfolio theory. Trust me, I've spent enough time working in the markets, unlike Ulrich. These lecturers want to scare you into thinking their subject's dead difficult just to make themselves look like less of a loser."

"OK, maybe, but I still need to learn this damned thing now."

"Indeed, but that's why I'm here isn't it?"

Here being Marianna's student bedroom. Whilst it may lack the opulence of a five star hotel, consisting as it does of a meagrely proportioned but neatly made-up single bed, study table and chair and antiquated sink, it's still a venue any red-blooded male would consider a prime location. The next hour I spend helping her goes quick. I flirt a bit, she learns a bit. Marianna's a smart girl. She smells good too, like she's wearing body lotion. Probably put it on after she's worked out and showered. I'm getting distracted, the only place we can sit is on her bed and my flirting's getting clumsier and more suggestive. She's acting a bit cooler now; realise I'm flogging a dead horse here. Time for a swift exit, there's somewhere else I want to be.

"Anyway, I've got to shoot off now, I'm meant to meet someone. I'll call you and we'll pick up on this again later in the week."

She comes to her door and kisses me quickly on the cheek. On the way out I get to thinking that Marianna's a really nice kid. I mean she's hot and she knows it but she handles it well, doesn't play on it. Is she the hottest babe on the course? In all honesty no, that honour has to go to Simone Sanders, as officially voted number one in the MBA (that's as in Measured by Boobs and Ass) count-down in one of our male bonding sessions. Marianna polled well. There was clear blue water between her and Petra Kominski from the Ukraine who scored heavily in the ass department but fell away a little elsewhere. But in the end there was only ever one winner, Simone. Obviously I've set my lecherous little heart on gaining carnal knowledge of all three by the course end, but to date progress has been disappointing. At least with the top two. Petra can wait. Little problem of accessibility with Simone. Basically I can't get any, even when a chance came, my performance was well below par.

"Hi, it's Simone isn't it? I'm Harry. Don't think we've spoken before. So how you finding things so far?"

We're in a lift together about a month ago. She's wearing tight black trousers and a fitted red cashmere jumper, tasty. It's the first time I've got Simone on her own, a moment of truth.

"It's a little slow. If this is only a one year programme, they need to maintain momentum."

She starts ruffling through her leather bag before pulling out her lipstick.

"Yeah, right. Anyway, I notice you worked in equity sales in the States. I worked in fund management in the City before coming here, I'd love to have dinner with you and…"

She looks at me for the first time with what might just be a flicker of interest.

"So, who did you work for in the City exactly?"

"KCT, they're a Belgian bank."

"Never heard of them. You like run a hedge fund there or something?"

"Ran a kind of mutual fund, UK equities."

She looks distinctly unimpressed at this disclosure and turns her attention back to the contents of her bag, retrieving a small mirror and then concentrating on applying a serious coating of scarlet lipstick. Then she looks up briefly as the lift door opens.

"Oh, right. Anyway, I gotta run. See you around."

So that was it, my first and so far last personal conversation with Simone. Of course I've ogled her from a distance like we all have. I mean what's not to fancy? She's a tall, I'd say good 5'7", blonde, tanned, gym-buffed, teeth-bleached all-American babe. Best of all she isn't a Park Avenue princess, try as she might. Nope, Simone still has that little hint of small town alpha female about her. In short, you know she's had to work just that little bit harder to get on in life and just imagine what that could mean in the bedroom.

Of course, as a Brit my antennae weren't quite as tuned to these things initially, but you pick up on them quick enough, at least if like me, you look for any scrap of information to tilt things that marginal degree in your favour. That'd been how I earned my living, and a good one too, before I came here. I mean, it was the mother of all bull markets and anyone who had a pulse and could talk the talk could make money. Then things got a lot harder. Basically the market was fucked along with pretty much anyone working in it. I hung in there better than most, managing by stealthy political manoeuvring to survive the first two culls. Long nights of team building and client arse kissing yielding dividends. Then October 2002, a market that had been haemorrhaging losses just gave up. I got tannoyed.

"Will Harry Stanton please report to the fifth floor immediately. That's Harry Stanton to the fifth floor please."

Classy. That's it, grab your personal effects, along with any stuff that might prove useful in the future. Respond with derision to their initial pay-off offer, call your solicitor, then get to the pub for a post-mortem with the rest of the refugees.

"No point staying on anyway, compliance crawling all over us for shorting stocks PA. Looking at zero bonus for the first time in twelve years. Tell you, Noah, this game's fucked. Way my fund's been performing was only a matter of time before I got carried out."

"So what now? Hedge fund? Sell-side?"

"Maybe, I mean I'm thirty-one, got a bit of cash put away. Don't know if I can be arsed with it all for a while."

"Thought about an MBA?"

"Go back to college? You're fucking joking!"

"Seriously, Harry, my brother-in-law did one. Went to the States for two years. Said it was a piece of piss. He's living over there now. Good job on Wall Street and shacked up with some sexy undergrad chick."

"Seriously? Never thought of the shagging potential. Don't fancy the life of a student again much though."

"Who said anything about living like a student? Visited Melvin a couple of times, had his own apartment, brought over his Plasma and Bang & Olufsen and all his other gear. Tell you, mate, he said it was like being on holiday for two years. Best of all no-one gives you any grief for it. In fact, it's the opposite: our whole bloody family were singing his praises for doing it."

"Yeah? Doesn't sound too shabby, might have to look into it. Nice one, mate. Anyway, what you up to next?"

"Off to do my sailing skipper's certificate. Buy my own yacht and skipper it off the Cayman Islands. Been a dream for years. Only reason I put up with this shit for so long."

Fair play to Noah. Used his inalienable right as a black man in a white man's world to up his payment to almost half a million. No need to even mention the words 'racial' and 'discrimination', the very mention of the lawyer he was retaining proving sufficient. Got an e-mail from him the other day, sent from a yacht in the Caribbean. I'm sure the picture of him being served a bottle of

Legends beer by a bikini wearing babe wasn't meant to make me jealous.

More I thought about what he said afterwards, more it made sense. I'm thirty-one years old with no discernable skills, expensive tastes, a complete lack of personal morality, inestimable self-belief and an aversion to hard work. An MBA could save me going through the motions of looking for non-existent equity fund management jobs, give the market a year to recover, be talked up appropriately to gullible employers and best of all allow me to indulge my favourite pastime, myself. As an added bonus, the course didn't even start for almost a year, giving me the perfect excuse to blow large sums of cash on trivial pursuits without taking any crap for it. On that note, the timing of my departure from the City had been rather unfortunate meaning I'd miss the December party season. The month when little or no work is done, multiple piss-ups are held with all the attendant opportunities for sexual conquests, information gathering on colleagues and clients, settling of personal vendettas incurred during the year and all the other little delicious treats of the season of goodwill. Still a trip to Thailand more than compensated for these lost opportunities. Sexual harassment is unfortunately beginning to permeate down the professional scale nowadays and some of these new graduates are surprisingly clued up on such matters. Not a situation pertaining in the fleshpots of Phuket, I'm pleased to say. So much for globalisation.

Anyways, a bit of R&R in the East, then back home to a pile of glossy brochures all offering me the opportunity of a lifetime to 'make a quantum leap', 'gain the clarity to triumph', 'learn without frontiers' or 'seize my future'. All of course providing I could render the necessary five figure sum. Quick guide to choosing an MBA the Harry Stanton way: if they charge a fee to apply, fuck 'em (money grabbing mercenaries); ask you to write a dozen essays to persuade them to sell you a place – life's too short; course lasts more than a year – bin the brochure, too much opportunity cost, (hey, I sound like one already); requirement to write answers to vague and essentially meaningless open ended questions, (sample: 'describe a moral dilemma you have faced and how you resolved it') – perfect, apply immediately! Any school that affords so much opportunity to sell oneself by engaging in meaningless generics is fine by me. Certainly augurs well for 'the MBA experience'.

Of course once I arrived at University, I dragged myself along to the freshers' fair event where all the various clubs were touting their wares. A cursory glance was all that had been required to discern that no bloody way I was joining any of the MBA societies. I mean entrepreneurship, that's taking the piss; someone wants to start a business, they don't exactly go back to University. Anyway, the choice elsewhere is much more to my tastes, although even there I am distressed to learn that some individuals will be wasting three years worth of invaluable leisure time on pursuits such as the Investment Society. I mean, would you employ anyone who spent their spare time as a student comparing the differing implications of international accounting standards? Darts? Now that's another matter, actually quite fancy that, used to take clients to the World finals at the Lakeside, but will have to be very much a secondary pursuit due to unfavourable gender demographics. Sailing? That offers possibilities, mind you this is England, not exactly the Caymans where my old friend Noah is hanging out. Polo? Nope, going to be full of Argentineans and Australians, too much competition for the ladies' affections. Hang on a minute, what's this? Two young bits of totty clad in tight jodhpurs and knee-high boots, the Hunt Society. Now this has real potential, excellent marketing effort, shame they're not carrying whips though! Twenty minutes of flirtatious conversation later and I'm a fully signed up member, via Gold Amex, of course. Such a good sign when a student society accepts one. No experience of horse riding, naturally, but that's irrelevant - it's the Hunt Balls I'm interested in. Black tie, champagne and young, impressionable drunken girls. Now that, I do have plenty of experience in.

The actual course itself is proving a breeze. I've done the CFA exams through work, which covers Finance and Accounting, and most of the rest of the stuff's just psycho-babble. Being such an altruistic soul, I've been delighted to be able to offer academic assistance where appropriate. The appropriateness being determined by the sex and looks of the individual requiring assistance; hence my helping Marianna understand the practical implications of the Capital Asset Pricing model. Unfortunately, I'm so helpful she's told a couple of her friends. Recently, I've also found myself hosting revision sessions in the cheap hotel lobby style environment which constitutes our common room. Understandably, this change of venue does not encourage Marianna to feel relaxed enough to wear the skimpy pyjamas she favours in her study bedroom. Of course, the realisation that devotion to Carlos, her boyfriend back home, means lingering glances of Marianna's honey dew thighs, not to mention the numerous photos of herself in a bikini on the bedroom wall, are as far as I'm likely to get does force me to diversify my efforts elsewhere.

Thankfully, this has proven fruitful, particularly amongst the undergraduate population, and the decision to join the Hunt Society proves an inspired one as evidenced by events at the Hunt

Ball. The turnout amongst the young ladies was heart-warming, made even better by the bunch of fools who constituted their male counterparts. The latter were split into two distinct categories: chinless wonders who'd clearly rather be rogering each other; and thrusting young blades who undoubtedly would provide some competition in years to come but for now lacked experience and, in particular, an ability to handle alcohol. I had, of course, spent a little time on the Internet prior to attending the Ball, familiarising myself a little more with the pursuit of hunting. Not a difficult task. In fact, the posing of the question as to where I hunted was a golden opportunity to market myself. Allowing me, as it did, to explain that due to my highly successful, but extremely stressful career in the City, I hadn't been able to ride out as much as I would have liked in recent years. The MBA and its time demands were unfortunately precluding me from taking as active a role in the hunt as I had hoped this year, but I was delighted to be here on such a celebratory evening. By some perceptive questioning I was able to narrow the field down to a couple of possibilities. Henrietta, twenty and blonde from Shropshire, just had the edge over Theresa, nineteen and brunette from Essex. In fairness it was a close call, Theresa was shorter with fewer generations of money behind her (I'd guess two at most, more likely one), but she had bumps in all the right places and was definitely one for the future, provided she was knocked back very delicately. Which, of course, she was, straight into the arms of young Somerled who I'd met at the bar and cultivated for this very purpose. This left me free to enjoy the pleasures of the flesh with the beautiful and modestly pissed Henrietta.

Which is why I find myself pulling into the car-park at Theresa's halls of residence. Theresa, it has to be said, has proven a much more fruitful acquaintance than the frankly, rather disappointing, Henrietta, who proved to be much more pissed than I had first imagined. All situations are salvageable, however, and so this one proved, after managing to persuade Theresa that I had stepped back purely because I thought that she and Somerled were a couple. Now, having accepted defeat at Marianna's, I'm eagerly anticipating a little afternoon sex with Theresa, one of the great pleasures of student life, which only those of us who have worked for several years truly appreciate. Jumping out of the car, (bought on very favourable terms from my employer as part of my settlement), in eager anticipation, I notice a familiar figure approaching. Well, well, if it isn't the MBA chart-topper herself, the beautiful Simone, looking particularly tasty. Looks like I'm about to get a second bite at the cherry, although I've no idea why.

11

"Danny, man, you gotta start getting your head around some of this new slo-core stuff that's coming outta the East Coast. That early '90's English stuff was cool in its day, but times have changed, my friend."

The gospel according to my Brazilian amigo Miguel. Three years in Miami promoting an indie night at Churchill's pub, and he's a self-pronounced expert on the 'gaze scene. 'Course when he pitched up here to do his PhD on the appropriate capital structure for proprietors of modelling agencies, he reckoned without running into me: a dude who's dedicated the past decade of his life to the short-lived musical phenomenon that was Thames Valley shoegazing. Or, as famously described by the music press, 'the scene that celebrates itself'.

"Man, why waste time listening to something that ain't gonna cut it the way the old stuff does? It's opportunity cost, just like they teach us on my course."

"Opportunity cost my ass. Don't start quoting that crap to me, Danny. You're just lazy and tight. Any fool can download a lot of this new shit for next to nothing nowadays; you're one sorry ass dinosaur."

OK, so Miguel wants to step it up a level.

"So, dude, you're telling me none of the following made the play list at your little Wednesday night residency: Ride, Slowdive, Chapterhouse, Moose, the Valentines, Lush, Spaceman 3, Whipping Boy…"

"Whipping Boy are Irish, my friend, as technically are the Valentines. And strictly speaking they're not really shoegazers; more a kind of post-rock vibe. Anyway, correct me if I'm wrong here, Danny, but wasn't it you who told me that true shoegazing began and ended with Slowdive's 12-inch debut: the imaginatively titled, 'Slowdive'?"

"You're taking me out of context here, dude. What I meant was that it was the epoch of the genre. The other bands still made a valid contribution, they just didn't define the moment."

"Danny, mate, you're so full of shit. How the fuck did they ever let a loser like you in here in the first place?"

Miguel's laughing at this but tell you the truth it's a question I've been asking myself ever since I got here. I get up to change the record on the turntable as it's my choice now. Time to hit him with a classic: Chapterhouses's debut, 'Whirpool', complete with guest appearance by Rachel Goswell on stand-out track, Pearl. Made John Peel's festive fifty that year: 1991, I believe. I've got a shit-eating grin on my face at Miguel's pathetic attempts not to acknowledge just what a kick-ass tune this is.

Cool dude, Miguel. He saw me come into the pub one evening beginning of term, when we were having a kind of getting to know you gig with the PhD students, with a bag of vinyl from a trip to Rough Trade in Notting Hill. 'Course most of the PhD's act like they're there to save capitalism from itself, whereas most of our gang like to think they're its Praetorian Guard. No matter, pretty much everyone else there, MBA and PhD alike, probably thought I was mentally retarded carrying a bag of plastic. Miguel, though, dug the fact I liked to listen to my music the only true way: through the grooves. We got rapping and turns out we had something in common. 'Course once we realised we actually had similar tastes in music we've spent the entire time since denigrating the finer points of each other's. So here we are, just kicking back, having a smoke and listening to some old school 'gaze. Suddenly my mobile goes; it's Simone Sanders, real hot chick off the course. Wonder why she's calling me?

"Danny sweetie, I'm like soooo stressed, can you drive over here with a little weed and we can chill? Come on, be an angel."

"Simone, Hi. Sure, I'd love to hang out with you, but Miguel's here. Why don't you come over and join us; we're just hanging out smoking and listening to some music."

Man, that doesn't go down well. She reminds me that I told her earlier in term just to call me any time she wanted to hang out. Well, now she wants to hang out, but at her place, 'cause she wants quality time with me.

"I guess so. I mean, I'd be delighted to come hang out with you, Simone Where's your dorm room?…Oh right… OK, sure I know where that is. I'll be over in like forty minutes… OK, sure, I'll leave right now then, no sweat."

Miguel's looking a bit pissed; think he's got an idea what's going down here.

"So, what's happening? You bailing out man?"

"Sorry dude, I need to be somewhere. Listen, we can pick this up again later…"

"Screw that. Who was that, anyway?"

"Simone from the MBA. You know her, she's…"

"What the fuck you wanna go and hang out with her for? She's a grade A bitch, man. You think you gonna get anywhere with her, you're sorely mistaken. Better believe she just wants you for something."

I just shrug my shoulders. It's a bit lame bailing on Miguel like this, but Simone, well, she don't seem like the sorta girl who takes no for an answer. Plus, she is hot: you never know, share a little smoke maybe get to know her a little better. Deep down, below the teak-tough exterior, I think maybe she's looking for a sensitive guy like me.

Miguel collects his vinyl, picks up his stash and leaves. Say I'll call him later, but he needs to do some work on his paper. Know we'll kiss and make up over a spliff. Don't usually smoke dope with people from the business school other than Miguel. I mean some of these MBA types - whole different zoological species to the rest of humanity. Most of 'em don't do drugs and the ones that do are mainly coke fiends. Good old weed is just too chill for them; scared it'll make them into environmentalists or something. I don't do coke; nope, nice bag of draw and Danny's at peace with the world. Simone though, she's a good time girl. Had me sussed right from the first time we met. Asked me if I knew where she could buy some Rizla paper. Tell her just to let me know any time she wants a smoke; always got a little spare to share with friends. The smile I get in return, coupled with the "thank-you sweetie" and squeeze on the knee as we're seated at the pub table may sound banal, but it gave me a feeling I'll bet my life most men never have; the kind that only comes from having the gratitude of a beautiful woman.

So I get up, take Reading's finest off the turntable. Sorry, Rachel, you're still the one for me but duty calls. Pull on my fleece and am about to leave then think, hang on - this is a one-to-one audience with the gorgeous Simone. So, I change my shirt, fix my hair, put on my leather jacket and swallow half a packet of tic-tacs. Am too stoned to drive so need to grab a cab; decide to walk to the rank rather than call one. Traffic's pretty heavy so took a bit longer than I thought, but now I'm outside Simone's place. Pretty modest from the outside, but has its own entrance so guess it's not a dorm room or flat share like most of the rest of us. Anyway, I ring the buzzer and she's at the door in a second.

"Danny sweetie, so good to see you."

But she's looking behind me as she says it, sees the taxi pull off. What's her problem man, she's glaring at me like I've screwed up or something!

"Where's your damn car, Danny? I need the motherfucker to move some stuff".

Simone Sanders

Of course I'd already decided who to call beforehand: that stoner, Danny. Real loser, Canadian or something, so what d'you expect? Remember getting stuck beside him at a table in a bar early in term. Asked what he did in his spare time and he starts giving me some hard-luck story about how his daughter lives couple hundred miles away, somewhere called Manchester. Said he drives up there when he can, so made a mental note at the time that he must have a car. Then he starts asking me if I'm a lesbian. Say what? Least that's what I thought he meant when he asked whether I'd checked out the gay scene in San Francisco. Turns out he meant some stupid shit called the 'gaze scene. Something to do with this music he's into. Cut him dead there. One of my cardinal rules is to never get involved with artistic types, surefire bet you'll end up with a dead-head who'll drag you round town on public transport, stopping in every seedy shithole of a bar with a welfare friendly door policy. Danny's sole topics of conversation that night revolved around this dumb-sounding music I'd never heard of, his daughter and smoking grass. Still, life's taught me it's always worth spending five minutes on everyone, even losers like him. So dropped a few hints, leaving him thinking I was into grass too. As if. Haven't touched that stuff since junior year undergrad. Simone is one drug and alcohol free individual. I mean obviously there was the Prozac last year and coke at times of professional necessity, of course, and well maybe just the odd glass of champagne to appear sociable. That's the thing about the British, they're a nation of fuckin' alcoholics. You have to drink to fit in. Couldn't believe it when I first arrived. These guys just drown what little ambition and talent they have in a sea of booze, even the supposedly smart ones. Makes them easy pickings of course. Want to control a study group full of Brits? Easy, just schedule it for 8am. Even better if it's on the weekend: they'll acquiesce to anything just to get through it quickly. That's if they even turn up.

Danny finally turns up, clearly stoned, in a fuckin' taxi, no way! I'm stuck with this lame-ass dork, stoned, car-less and expecting to sit here and smoke dope with me. What the fuck was I thinking of anyway, relying on him? That ridiculous little beard thing on his chin shoulda warned me that he'd screw up. Shit, this sucks the big one. I'm going to struggle to make the study group at all now. Damn, that could cost me some marks in this ridiculous peer group marking exercise this place insists on. Fuck, nothing for it but to get another car out here. Although this is a small self-contained apartment, it's in a block and you never know who's gonna call round. Those damn dogs will start to smell before long. They've gotta go, like now.

Racking my brains to think who else has a car when a big black SUV pulls into the car-park. Some guy comes swaggering out of it looking pretty pleased with himself. He's a bit older and better dressed than the dorks you usually see round here. In fact, I'm sure he's on the course. Harry? Henry? Something like that. Haven't had a lot to do with him; tried to hit on me once but it was a half-assed attempt. From what I've heard, he treats this as a year out from the real world, an excuse to party and sleep with girls half his age. In fact, that must be what he's doing here, as come to think of it, I've noticed that car parked here before in the morning. Not hard really - it sure stands out in that company. Shit, I don't really know this guy but right now he's the only game in town. Time to introduce myself properly.

Harry Stanton

"Hey, Harry! How you doing? Listen I'm kinda stuck; I need to schlep some stuff out of here and I don't have a car. Look could you help me just for 10 minutes? I'll be like, so grateful. I'd just ask to borrow the car but you guys drive on the wrong side of the road, and I'd hate to risk a crash as it's such a beautiful car. It's a BMW right?"

Damn she's sexy: brown trousers, cropped white shirt, tied just above a washboard stomach; but it's the hand on hip pose that clinches it. Effortless really.

"Yeah, it's an X5. Listen, what do you need to move? I've got golf clubs in the back so not sure how much room there is, but I'll be delighted to try to help if I can."

"It's two bin-liner bags. I'll be honest; it's my ex's stuff, Harry. I found out the bastard was cheating on me and dumped him. Then he starts rumours about me sleeping around. I'm real upset. I just need to get rid of his stuff; he hurt me real bad. I can't bear being reminded of him. Please help me Harry. Everyone says you're a good guy. Most of the people with cars I know are his friends. I can't ask them. I'm just a bit vulnerable at the moment."

God, now she's starting to sniffle and I'm getting all kind of sexual cravings just looking at the pleading look in her eyes. Almost let her beg a little longer but decide to play the good guy. This situation has definite potential. Theresa can wait.

"Sure no probs, it's cool. Are the bags upstairs?" She nods, sobbing. "Then let me help you load the car. We'll have you sorted in no time."

She nods agreement and leads the way towards what must be her apartment; looks like one of those flats for married couples. Make a quick appraisal when we get inside. Pretty tidy really; couple of those idiotic self-help books scattered on the glass coffee table, release the power of your innate self in thirty days and all that crap. No sign of any blokes' stuff though. Good. Look for any tell-tale photos of square-jawed GQ types but there's only a family shot: two adults and a couple of kids. Must have been taken a long time ago judging by the bloke's sideburns. The young girl in the photo looks about six or seven, has that willing to please expression on her face that kids sometimes do. Hear someone clearing their throat behind me and realise I'm not alone. Turn around and recognise this scruffy looking guy from the course - Danny, think he's Canadian. I remember him because one night, early in the first month, when we were doing the whole tedious getting to know you thing, we got talking. Anyway, this clown finds out I'm from Reading and starts banging on about a couple of bands from the town that he's really into. Apparently, they had a real cult following back in the early '90s. Told him I'd never heard of them as was away at Leeds University at the time. Funny thing is I remember my younger brother was into them after he mentions it. Shoegazing, that's right. Michael used to have posters on his wall, these pale, weird-looking fuckers with floppy hair. I exchange grudging pleasantries with Danny, then we go into a tiny kitchen where there're several diet books stacked on the shelf but no sign of any food alongside them. Simone's standing in the doorway behind us.

"That's his stuff on the floor, in those bin bags. They're pretty heavy; he had a lot of shit like guys do. Best if you guys take an end each and carry them out one at a time."

Me and this Danny bloke look at each other and shrug. He takes one end, I take the other. Fuck, this stuff's heavy. We carry it through the lounge. I make an attempt at conversation.

"Fuck me, this guy must have had a hell of a stash of porn, judging by the weight of this."

He half-smirks. This guy doesn't appear too pleased at my presence here. Also, unless I'm very much mistaken, he's stoned. This is a weird set-up. I open the boot door, shift some stuff around and we heave the bag in. After one more trip with the world's greatest conversationalist, we're done. Now where to?

17

So I'm here on Simone's doorstep, but I'm sure not getting the welcome I anticipated. She's pissed big time, and man is she letting me know it.

"Danny, be my friend please. Go back and get your car. I don't care how stoned you are. I need it, now!"

What the fuck is wrong with her? We can move the stuff any old time. This is one stressed chick. Talk about high maintenance, dude.

"But Simone, babe, let's just chill, we can move the stuff later. Let's kick back and have a smoke... mellow out together."

She looks as if she's about to lose it big time at this when all of a sudden she's distracted by something behind us. I look around and a black jeep kinda thing pulls into the car park. I recognise the driver; it's that guy from Reading, Harry. Real flash son-of-a-bitch. Tried to have a conversation once with him about the 'gaze scene, when I saw from the profile book he'd grown up in Reading, but he wasn't interested. Since then, we just nod now and again, two lives just brushing past each other. To be honest, it's like that with most people on the course. People get categorised pretty quickly: those that are worth knowing and those that aren't. It takes an investment in time to get to know someone and these dudes expect a dividend. Me, I just wanna get by. Only came here because I got the scholarship. Didn't expect to get that but they had quite a few on offer for public sector workers. Given I'd worked in local authority town planning in London for four years, I was eligible to apply. Guess I just thought, why not? My five-year-old daughter Caitlin's over here, living up in Manchester now. No way I'd get to see her if I went back to Canada. I was bored at work, so fuck it here I am, all fees paid and my job held open. Shit, it could be worse. Plenty of time to chill and after all, there aren't many chicks like Simone at the local authority offices in Croydon. Right now, though, Simone is one stressed individual and it has to be said, not a whole heap of fun to be around.

"OK Danny, what's this guy's name? Harry? Right, you go into the flat out of the damn way. Stay in the living room. I'm going to get him to help, OK."

And off she goes to talk to Harry, who looks pretty made up to see her. Damn, her walk's as mean as her temper. Guess that's why I'm still here.

So, finally we load these goddamn bags into the car. Now I've got to come up with a plausible reason why we're dumping them in the river, then I'm home free. Usually I cover every base, but because I thought it was just that dumb-ass Danny, I hadn't prepared my story as carefully as I might have. Got to play the emotional wronged girlfriend angle, worked with that Harry guy before. He's obviously a sentimental wuss.

"Harry, I just can't bear to have these things around me a minute longer. It's breaking me up. Please take them to the river and we'll just throw them in and let them sink. Then I can start to get over this."

"OK. I mean, if that's what you want. There's the council dump not far from here. We could go there instead. It's up to you."

"Harry, the river just feels right; it feels like closure. I know I'm probably not making any sense, just be my friend please. I really need a friend right now."

He seems a bit doubtful, then dead-head Danny butts in.

"The river's kind of appropriate. It's like metaphorical. I mean the relationship has sank, let these final reminders sink with it. That's what you want, isn't it Simone?"

You're shitting me! Why didn't I think of that? This joker actually has his uses.

"Danny darling, you're so right. I guess subconsciously that's what I was trying to say, it's just so hard to express what I feel at the moment. The river's only a couple of blocks away, we can just find a quiet spot and ditch the bags."

So off we drive; ten minutes later we're there. On the way, Harry's making heavy-handed attempts to flirt with me. Danny's just sitting there looking uncomfortable; whatever. I use the excuse of being upset over my imaginary boyfriend's infidelity as cover for ignoring them. It's a windy, damp afternoon, the kind that England seems to specialise in at this time of year. Depressing, with no redeeming features. Bit like most of the student body here. Eventually, we find a quiet spot. I pass it every day when I'm running. Only one shitty old car there, which looks like it's been abandoned. There's a little wharf, the guys drag the bags out along it and throw them into the river where it looks pretty deep. I'd put weights in there so the dogs will sink quickly and stay sunk, least long enough for it not to matter if they're found. Anyway, they weren't electronically tagged and I'd removed all their ID. I only bought them two months ago

19

when I first came here and found out these assholes wouldn't let me have a gun. It's not like anyone's gonna miss them. Certainly not the guys I bought them off, couple of South Africans I met on the train to London one Saturday afternoon at the beginning of term. Was on my way down to hook up with some former hedge fund client of mine who was in London for the weekend. The guy's a plank but he's got cash and contacts and I know he'll stand me a decent dinner. Anyway, like what else was I gonna do on a Saturday night - go to the student union bar? So my head's buried in a text book, usual bone dry bullshit that almost breaks your goddam arm carrying around, when a can of beer lands in my lap.

'Hoesit girl? Want something from the bottle store, ya?"

"Actually I'm all set for now, thanks."

"You from States, hey?'

I tried to ignore them but they were drunk off their ass and pretty insistent with it. Sometimes it's easier just to talk to people like that. At least that way you can try and control the conversation.

"Yeah, San Francisco."

"San Fran hey, now that's a lekker dorp. Lot of poofters though, so what you doing in England hey?'

'I'm studying for an MBA actually.'

"No shit! Me and the ous here, we're on like a rugby trip, spend most of the time on the dagga though…Deutsche over there, he lives here, don't you man.'

This red-faced man mountain staggers over.

"Ya man, breed the dogs man. Best damn dogs in the country, no shit. You want a guard dog, you come speak to Deutsche, hey that right my broer?'

'It's true man. Damn Dobermans are lekker mean.'

I get to thinking of all the stories I've heard on the radio of murders and shit. In fact, there's a newspaper lying on the seat opposite, Daily Express or something. Had quick read of it when I got on. I tell you this country sounds worse than the States. Maybe I could use a little protection now that I'm all on my own. I mean, I've got my pepper spray but that's not gonna stop a rapist. So I get this Deutsche guy's number just before a football is produced leading to a mass brawl. Turns out he lived near-by and true to his word did have some goddamn mean Dobermans for sale. Bummer the University wouldn't let me keep them but reckon I'll get by OK. Turns out this country's pretty safe if you stick to what you know.

The whole disposing of the bodies deal only takes about five minutes and it's job done, as they say over here. Do like that phrase; think it's one I'll use back home.

Harry Stanton

"OK, that's the past over with Simone. How about you and I go for a drink? Danny, I'll drop you off at the business school if you like?"

"Harry, you've been such a sweetheart and I'm like so grateful and everything, and of course I'd love to have a drink with you guys, but you know what my study group are like. They're such a bunch of ball-breakers. I don't show up, I'm screwed."

Which is more than I'm gonna be, at least by Simone. May as well play the long game here, get rid of laughing boy as well. He looks as pissed off as I feel. Reckon she's played us both here. Won't be happening to me again, I can tell you.

"I guess your ex was one of those rich dudes with all kinds of shit he didn't need Simone?"

"What the fuck are you asking me that for?...Sorry Danny, that was rude. I'm still just a bit raw. Yep, he did. We were together for a while."

"So, he like moved over here with you then, I guess?"

"Huh...yeah, he did. Just didn't work out though...Listen do you mind if we don't talk about it. In fact we're almost at the school - just drop me off here."

I drop them both off. Simone thanking me curtly, Danny grunting. Last time that dope-head's riding in my car. Then, head over to Theresa's. She's still there, and accepts heartfelt apologies for my late arrival, together with the compensatory bottle of Lanson I've picked up on the way. Had hoped it'd be a bottle of Krug with Simone, but you gotta play the hand your dealt, know what I mean? Been a funny old day really, but when Theresa proudly shows me the freshly inked tattoo of a little butterfly on her left hip, I think it's one that's definitely ending well.

Danny McMullen

"Maybe have that smoke we talked about later Simone. Should I call you, or..."

"Sorry, too busy."

And she's off down the road without so much as a good-bye. I'm pissed at how this afternoon turned out. I mean, what the hell was I doing out there in the rain throwing bags of Simone's ex-boyfriends shit into the river when I coulda been back toking and listening to 'gaze with Miguel? And for what? To be treated like I'm not even there. I'm still a bit hazed and just wanna get out of here, go back home and chill. Had enough of miss Simone Sanders for one day. Maybe I'm being a bit hard on her though. I mean, she just split from her boyfriend and all that. Must kinda suck moving all the way over here with him and then finding out he was cheating on her. I mean, it's not like I don't know what it's like to be screwed over by someone you care about. That's life though man, shit happens. I'm gonna go home, skin up and listen to Swervedriver.

Chapter Two

Simone Sanders

D amn, this day is gonna drag. I mean, presentation skills. C'mon, like I need that kinda bullshit. Working in the brokerage business you learn that when you pitch stock, you pitch yourself, simple as. But here I am, stuck in this shitty classroom on a goddamn Saturday, about to listen to some bunch of underachievers trying to learn how to do what should come naturally: sell themselves. Anyway, looks like we're ready to roll, the professor running this little show just appeared, but, ohmigod, would you take a look at what he's brought with him.

"Guys, this is Norman Spiers. Norman's an actor. He's going to help us to relax in front of the camera so we can portray ourselves naturally. A key skill of all good presenters, I hope you'll agree."

This Norman dude, who looks like some kinda sixties throwback with his ponytail, denim shirt and black jeans, is grinning and giving us the thumbs up. Like this guy's gonna help me sell myself; get the fuck outta here.

"OK gang, to-day's all about you. By the end of it you're going to think of the camera as your friend. Presenting to a room full of people is going to feel as natural as hosting a dinner party. In fact it'll be a lot easier because you won't even have to clear up afterwards, ha-ha."

Jesus, what a loser. Even the professor looks embarassed.

"Guys, I'm gonna disappear now and leave you all with Norman. I'll pop back later in the day for a progress report."

Yeah right, no way was one of our precious academics giving up his Saturday for this bullshit. Rather pay some outta work hippy a few dollars and charge us royally for the privilege. Time to get with the plan here.

"So Norman, like we've all got real busy schedules here. You reckon we can get this finished up by say noon?"

"I'm sorry you're not wearing a name tag. May I ask your name?"

"Simone."

"Thanks Simone. I don't like name tags myself, too institutionalised. In fact, why don't we all take them off then we

23

can go around the room and introduce ourselves properly. Sound like a plan?"

"Hey Norman, think you could like, answer my question?"

"Sorry Simone, remind me what it was again?"

"I asked if we could get finished up by noon? We're all under a lot of time pressure here."

"I'm afraid not Simone. Were you not told? This is an all day programme. I'll do my best to get it wound up by six, so you guys can still have your evening though. That cool?"

Cool, six pm; what fucking planet is this guy on?

"No, that's not cool, Norman. I'm afraid that our schedules are way too busy to allow us the luxury of a full day fooling around in front of a camera. I'm sure the rest of my classmates will back me up on this."

Look around the room at the random four I've been subjected to this monumental waste of time with. Only one of them's in my study group – Balbeck– know he'll play ball. I so much look at the guy and he nearly has a seizure. The other three I dunno so well, one of them though, big guy, outta shape, name-tag says Sean McCollum, starts talking.

"Hold on there a minute Simone, this is pretty important stuff, we should get the most out of the day, like. Let's just go along with what the man here says."

What kinda goddamn accent is that, Scottish or something? Sounds a bit like that Irish guy they used to show on the TV back home with the beard and glasses. Some kinda politician I think, not that I paid much attention. Then, this Indian looking guy, Anand, chimes in.

"Yes, I think it's important we show a proper commitment to this exercise. We should not be so hasty in dismissing it as irrelevant."

Look around and there appears to be general agreement on this. Even Balbeck's nodding his head; least he is until I glare at him, then he kinda shrinks down into his seat and looks even more insignificant. Whatever, looks like I'm gonna have to go along with this. Game plan has to be to get my shit out of the way early on, then clear on out of here.

"Of course I take this seriously guys, I'm just asking for some kind of timeline for the day."

Norman's standing there with a smug grin on his face. This loser belongs in the soup kitchen, not an MBA classroom.

"OK then, why don't we crack on. First off, we'll all have an opportunity to present to camera. I know you've all been asked to prepare something. Then we'll play it back and we can all chip in with some observations. Sound cool? Any volunteers to open the batting?"

What's that mean? Shit, just as I realise and stick my hand up I'm beaten to it by fat Sean. Goddamn English, think they could use a language we can all understand.

"Sure, I'm up for it. It's Sean by the way. Just take this nametag off and I'll get cracking."

So Norman, the hippy, explains the deal. Idea is stand up and present for five minutes on a topic of our choice which we're meant to have prepared, then sit down and we all tell each other how much we sucked up there, or as Norman puts it 'engage in constructive criticism'. Sean's off and running while Norman videos the whole thing. He's rambling on in that impenetrable accent about something called fly-fishing. Apparently it's an exercise in tranquillity, patience and timing. Whatever, all his description of it's doing is putting my feet to sleep. These hard plastic seats are fucking uncomfortable on the ass as well. Going to have to interrupt here.

"Guys, excuse me but can we like open a window please? I'm falling asleep here."

Sean shakes his head but Norman says sure thing; it's a hot day for November.

Thing is I had a bit of a late one last night and I'm starting to feel a bit frazzled. Some of the girls had a get-together. Musta been some kinda mistake 'cause they'd left me out of the original e-mailed invitation, but heard a couple of them talking about it in the coffee bar. Obviously they were real apologetic when they realised they'd forgotten to invite me. Apparently the point of the evening was to plan the end of term party, 'course we never got round to that. Too busy having a blast. I probably had a glass or two too many of the champagne though, and, well it being a Friday night and all that, I did indulge in a little bit of the other. Very naughty, I know, but honest to God the pressure we're under here. Anyway, it was a fun evening, although I did have to let the manager know his staff's attitude sucked. I mean, that's one of the things about the Brits they just don't understand: the concept of customer service. Get blown off and they just suck it up, well screw that. OK, so maybe I created a bit of a scene when I demanded the manager take the service charge off the bill after that dumb-ass bitch of a waitress was rude to me. But what's it got to do with her if I don't want a main course? Price they charge for a starter I can sit there all night. Like I told the others, back in the States we wouldn't stand for that crap.

Finally Sean sits down and then for some weird reason this Japanese dude, who up until now hasn't said a word, starts clapping

25

and then the others join in. Sean's face goes even redder than normal and he lumbers over to his seat, sits his fat ass down and starts gulping from the stainless steel coffee bucket he's brought with him. Gross.

"OK gang, thanks to Sean for kicking us off, now any comments?"

There's a series of meaningless platitudes about how they enjoyed learning about fly-fishing, like what's enjoyable in learning about that? Few minor comments on how he could try not to use his hands so much, that kind of thing. About to move onto the next presenter but screw this, don't like this guy much anyway. Remember he argued with me in class a couple of weeks ago, when he was trying to promote that corporate social responsibility bullshit they go in for here. Kept making snide remarks about American corporations and how they screw over their workers. Like that's something we don't know?

"Just to give some feedback before we move on."

Norman looks like an excited puppy. Sean glances at Anand and half-smirks. So this gut-bucket thinks I'm a joke does he?

"Sure Simone, engage."

My pleasure.

"We're here to learn how to project a positive image of ourselves, right Norman?"

"Well, that comes with being a confident presenter but…"

"OK. Then, and don't take this personally, Sean you need to lose some serious weight."

"What'd you just say?"

"Sean, be honest with yourself. Like Norman says, appearance counts in business and well frankly, yours needs some work."

"What business of yours is it how I look? Everyone knows you're…"

"OK guys, let's just step back and relax here. Simone, I don't think the aim of this exercise is to engage in criticism that can be taken personally, even if it wasn't intended that way, which I'm sure it wasn't."

Fuckin'A it was.

"Just to clarify what I meant Norman, as we all know the camera adds weight and, well, in Sean's case that's something already in plentiful supply. Least he could do is like dress in black or something, rather than that bright red soccer shirt."

"Jesus, can you believe this bitch, no wonder you're the fucking class pariah."

"You fat piece of shit, just what the fuck are you talking about?"

26

"I'm talking about the fact we've only been here two months and already no-one can stand you. Asked to the girls' dinner last night were you?"

"For your information I did have dinner with the girls last night and when we voted on the rankest guy on the course you won by a fuckin' mile, asshole."

"Ok, that's enough. I really must ask you two to stop disrupting what we're trying to achieve here."

"Yeah, well who gives a fuck what you're asking, fucking dumbass? You think Brad Pitt would have to come in here and do this shit?"

Dumb-ass Norman just stands there with his mouth open then turns and flounces out the door, slamming it behind him, drama queen. Realise I better get a grip on myself, reckon Sean's drawn the same conclusion whilst the other three just sit there, Anand's shaking his head and looking at me in a way I don't like, almost say something but need to keep a lid on it.

"This is not good, we should not have behaved like that, we are not children."

So Balbeck's got something to say now, yeah? Looks like he's not alone.

"Balbek is right, we are not here to argue with each other and cause insult and hurt. That is foolish and pointless and a waste of the educational opportunity we have been given here."

"Last time I checked, Anand, we weren't being given it, we were paying for it."

"Indeed Simone, which is all the more reason we should be taking full advantage of the opportunities we are paying for."

The other four nod at this, I'm getting bored with this now. Sanctimonious bullshit. Then the professor organising things comes back in, no hip 'let's pretend we're all colleagues' vibe now. Looks at us like we're a bunch of seventh graders.

"Right, Norman just informed me about what went on here. First of all, I'm very disappointed, particularly at you two..."

Glares at me and fat schmuck.

"...under the circumstances there appears no point continuing the class. Those of you who want to can rebook for a future date; those that don't fine. It's not assessed so we won't force you to take it. End of day it's your loss."

And he's out the door without so much as a good-bye. Sean shakes his head at me and mutters something under his breath as he gets up and leaves, followed by Anand and the Jap. Decide I better try and mend some fences with Balbeck, end of the day we are in the same study group.

"Sorry, that got a bit outta hand there. It's just all the pressure we're under. It like makes people do funny things, know what I mean?"

"Yes, I know what you mean. It is not good to fight with classmates though. We should all try to help each other."

"I'm cool with that. I mean, hey, we work well together in study group, you and me, right?"

He looks at me and smiles as he nods his head, then he looks right at me.

"Can I ask if there are other matters that are concerning you?"

"Like what?"

"Maybe like family. Do you miss them? I can understand if that is so. I miss my family back in Bishkek very much."

Where? And what the hell does he think he's doing dragging my family into this? Think I'm gonna sit here and discuss that kinda shit with this loser, that's off bounds buddy.

"My family's fine. Like I said, it's just the pressure here. Anyway, I better run, got chores to do. Later."

He just nods and smiles at me as I leave. Kinda freaky, I tell you. Like he knows stuff about me. No way, keep it steady, fucking coke paranoia. Best just get out of here. Look at my watch, only ten to twelve. Whoever said confrontation doesn't get results?

Chapter Three

Danny McMullen

S hit, man. I've gotta get out of here in the next ten minutes or I'm gonna miss the train.

"Guys, I'm afraid I'm gonna have to split. I'm sorry to bail on you like this but I need to be somewhere."

"Is it really important, Danny? We are a bit behind schedule here and tomorrow's the first class we have with this guy. We all heard what happened with the other stream this morning."

Couple people grimace at this comment from Charles Millington. Group leader and all-round gifted amateur. Hard to believe he's the same age as me.

"I heard that Samuel Wong just stood there for five minutes not speaking while this guy tore him apart. Apparently no-one's seen Samuel since the end of the class."

"Sarah, I'm scared for that to happen to me, please no."

It's OK, Nakata, we're in this as a group. We just need to make sure our preparation is sufficiently robust to withstand scrutiny. What do you think, Charles?"

"Completely agree, Sarah. Let's not allow our learning to be disrupted by a professor performing for the crowd. We're not here to massage his ego."

Dude, it's not the professor I want to see performing for the crowd - it's Mark Gardener. I mean, Mark fucking Gardener and he's gonna play some of the classics. Am meant to be meeting Miguel at the train station in twenty minutes but I'm not gonna make it unless I get outta here real quick.

"Uhm…guys I'm like meant to be in London tonight at a gig. It's shitty timing, I know, but this was arranged a month ago and I really don't want to miss it."

Look at Charles when I say this, it's gonna be his call. Before he can speak though Sarah Jenkins replies.

"So who you going to see Danny?"

"Mark Gardener. You've probably not heard of him: used to be in a band called Ride a few years ago. I've been a fan for a long time."

"Oh, right. Guess they must have been before my time. I suppose you should get going if it's important to you. None of us want this course to completely take over our lives."

"Thanks, Sarah. Look guys, I'll make the time up later. Really appreciate this, thanks."

They all nod and seem pretty cool with the whole thing. I mean it's not exactly like I'm a driving force behind the group effort.

"It's fine by us Danny, although I hope for your sake he doesn't call on you tomorrow in class."

I hope for my sake he doesn't too, Charles, but right now I don't really give a fuck. Tonight I'm gonna be watching the front man from one of the greatest 'gaze bands of all time performing a few feet away. It's been ten years since I last saw Mark Gardener, back when he was still with Ride. March 1992, Brixton Academy, on the Going Blank Again tour. The sound that night knocked my head back ninety degrees, lifted my feet clean off the floor. The intensity of the noise and the sheer human wall in front of me screwed up any chance of getting to the front. But I was bouncing up and down like the floor was a trampoline, the energy from the stage crashing through the crowd, smacking me in the face. Being there, soaked in sweat, bathed in strobe lighting, was mesmerising. 'Course it's a much smaller venue tonight and Mark's doing an acoustic set, but that's cool.

I'm out the door and running down the road. Get to the station same time as Miguel and the train even arrives on time. Once we're on it, Miguel suggests a beer from the trolley cart. Sure, why not? We each grab a bottle of Becks. Won't have too many as don't like to be too buzzed when I'm watching bands, particularly on a night like tonight. Train journey passes pretty uneventfully and Miguel and I josh each other a bit. He's ten years younger than me and never saw Ride live so I play the elder statesman. Always plays it cool, Miguel, but I can tell he's pretty up for this by the way he actually shuts up and listens when I tell him about classic 'gaze gigs I've been to. Dig this as makes a change from me being on the edge of other people's conversations. Asks me if I've thought any more about spinning the vinyl at the MBA end of term party. Doubt it; just some dumb idea I get when we smoke too much dope. Somehow, I don't think a bunch of MBA's are really gonna dig a sonic assault from My Bloody Valentine while they're discussing i-banking starting packages. Train gets into Kings Cross and we sprint to catch the tube to Angel where tonight's gig's going down. Get to the venue: it's a long narrow pub with a stage. Guess it probably holds about two hundred people, max. Miguel goes to the bar and orders a couple of beers, asks me if I want anything to eat. Tell him I'm fine. Place's still pretty empty, maybe twenty or thirty people there and we grab a seat while Miguel eats his food, offers me some of his nachos but I'm too hyped up to eat. What if no one turns up? Realise Miguel's asking my opinion on something.

"Sigur Ros? Slowdive for slow learners man."

He half-grins and half winces at this.

"Shifted a lot more vinyl though."

"So what? I'll take musical integrity over marketing spin anytime. Tell you, with the shit I'm learning on this MBA, if I'd been managing Slowdive they'd have been on the cover of fuckin' *Rolling Stone*."

"Yeah, Danny? You can't even manage to keep your own shit together, never mind anyone else's!"

"Thanks, Miguel! Like I haven't got enough people on my case without you starting."

"OK man, just chill. I'm only rapping with you. C'mon, I'll get you another beer".

"Sorry, Miguel. I'm just a bit on edge here in case no-one turns up."

"They totally will, Danny. The man's a legend."

I smile and nod at him. When he gets back from the bar we're chatting amiably but I'm looking over his shoulder at the door, willing people to arrive. Miguel's right though. About ten minutes later the place begins to fill up and I relax and slug back my beer. Get chatting to the dude next to me, says we just missed Mark sound-checking and he was awesome. Suddenly see a familiar figure moving through the crowd. I lose my train of thought in the conversation I'm having and watch as people come up to Mark and shake his hand; someone gives him a glass of red wine.

Miguel's nudging me and nodding his head in Mark's direction asking if that's him. Tell him, yeah man, that's him. Let's move up to the front before he comes on. Get up there and there's a handful of older dudes there about my age. Some of them are wearing suits, look like they've come straight off a trading floor. Few chicks around but this is a mostly male audience. Miguel goes to get another beer but I tell him I'm OK. The stage is pretty small and most people are standing back a bit, but me and a couple of these older guys, we're right up there hard against it. Finally, Mark comes on accompanied by a couple of younger dudes and they play a few tunes I don't know. The crowd listen politely but it's a low key kinda vibe. Then he plays an acoustic version of an old Ride tune, Taste, and the attention level goes up a notch, stays there for another classic, Vapour Trail. Then all of a sudden he's joined by

31

a couple of other guys, one of them's Loz Colbert, the drummer from Ride. It's more crowded at the front now but I'm in a prime spot as they plug their instruments in and play the opening chords of Dreams Burn Down. I'm standing there, looking up at Mark Gardener and Loz Colbert and it's like the past ten years never happened. I'm back at the gig in Brixton again and Karen, Caitlin, this course, everything in between just happened to someone else.

Chapter Four

Harry Stanton

"We value a strong moral compass, that's the key attribute we seek when we recruit from an MBA programme".

Sure, like anyone here really swallows that crap. Thing is, look around me at the intent gazes and hands furiously scribbling notes, and I reckon a lot of them do.

"Are you committed to equal opportunities as an employer then?"

Alice Archibald, boring, earnest and ugly. Talk about setting a question up on a plate. The recruitment chick positively radiates appreciation upon hearing this grovelling excuse for a question.

"Absolutely, excellent question and thank-you for raising it. Our consultancy thrives on diversity; it's an integral component in our drive for excellence. As we serve a heterogeneous range of clients it's of paramount importance our workforce reflects that. Anything else would be an abdication of our corporate responsibility to society as well as commercially naïve."

She must think we're the ones who are naïve.

"So, why do you place so much emphasis on A-level results? Surely that discriminates against students from working class backgrounds and ethnic minorities."

Ethel Akinbiyi, describes herself as Anglo-Nigerian. Now, normally it's fair to say Ethel and I would have differing viewpoints on the social issues of the day. Assuming that is, I had the slightest interest in sharing mine with her, but this is a fair question and this consultancy chick's looking decidedly uncomfortable.

"It's just one of the metrics we use to evaluate candidates; we find it a useful yardstick of future potential."

"But why? Surely you've read all the recent evidence that kids from backgrounds traditionally associated with low achievement can outperform more privileged students with higher A-level grades once they actually get to University. If the universities are finally beginning to wake up to this why aren't you?"

Consultancy chick's blushing now, her red face makes a nice ensemble with her white blouse and navy suit. Actually, find I quite fancy her now, bet that's what she looks like when she's getting a good seeing to. Look at the way the tips of her ears are glowing. Think I'll try and chat her up afterwards.

"Well, we take a number of factors into account and..ahm... well, A-levels are just one of them. Obviously we want the best candidates irrespective of background."

Evil Ethel's not letting her off the hook that easy though. Real Rottweiller is Ethel. Wouldn't fancy disappointing her in the bedroom, though given that she outweighs me by a good two stone you'd have to put a gun to my head to get me in there in the first place. Still, never say never: that's my motto, and that arse is built for comfort.

"So, do you have a socio-demographic and ethnic breakdown of your graduate and MBA level employees then?"

Consultancy chick's opening and closing her mouth like a goldfish that's jumped out of its bowl. Then just as things are getting interesting and the mood in the room's altered perceptibly on Ethel's side with people actually putting down their pens to pay attention, who do you think comes to her rescue?

"Actually, I think we've exhausted this particular area now. Given the international nature of our class I'm sure we'd all like to learn more about opportunities for global mobility within your organisation."

Ethel glares at Hilary Jenkins-Spires who avoids eye-contact with her after bailing out consultancy chick, though I swear Hilary reddens just a little under the intensity of Ethel's baleful stare. Shame this little cameo's over, these recruitment seminars are dull as dishwater, all mindless platitudes and meaningless soundbites. Fine when you're twenty-one but bugger all use when you're older than the person presenting. Only came along tonight because I bumped into Marianna who is wearing a faded denim skirt more accurately described as micro than mini. She persuaded me to come with the promise we'd go for a drink later. I'm not talking about the Waitrose own label stuff they'll be serving here afterwards when we get to mix with the bunch of smug overachievers the consultancy's brought along from their recent intake. Had a quick butchers earlier and there wasn't a half decent bit of totty amongst them. What kind of fucking incentive is that to join? This thing wraps up and then Marianna insists on networking for a while, needless to say she's getting schmoozed by a couple of consultancy blokes. One of them, tall, bland looking TV host type, is making her laugh just a little too much for my liking. Now she's bringing him over.

"Harry, this is Douglas. He's asking me what the bars around here are like. I said we were going for a drink and he should join us."

"You don't mind, do you Harry? It's just I studied here as an undergraduate myself and it's always good to revisit the old stomping grounds, see what's new and all that."

This is England in November and this guy's wearing a lemon polo shirt, what the fuck's that all about? I know Marianna's not exactly clad appropriately for our climate but given her legs that's an error of judgement I thoroughly encourage. I nod something noncommittal whilst he says he'll just retrieve his coat and Marianna pinches me on the arm.

"Harry, don't be such a spoilsport, he's a nice guy, says he can help me if I apply for the consultancy. You know I'm interested in working there. Come on, don't be a grouch."

I smile despite myself, never can stay pissed off when she's around. Back comes Douglas purring away in his posh Edinburgh brogue and off we troop to the pub, Marianna positioned in between us, the centre of both our universes right now. Decide against taking him somewhere upmarket, let the bastard slum it a bit if he's that keen on our company. The Wetherspoons on the high street should do the job, anyone wearing a lemon polo shirt in there's going to look a right cunt. We go in and I am delighted to glean a sour note on his face as he views my choice of venue. Not only is he wearing lemon, it looks like he's sucking on one as well. Marianna's pretty oblivious to all this and to the numerous lecherous glances she's attracting. Actually better get her out of the fucking way into a corner before some of the blokes in here come steaming in. I point them in the direction of an empty booth that at least allows a degree of privacy and take their drinks orders: small glass of white wine for her and a bottle of Corona for him. Must think he who drinks Mexican shags Mexican or something, fucking clown.

"That your bird then, mate? Fucking give her one, well fit ain't she."

Some care in the community case is addressing this to me at the bar. Bad clothes, bad skin, bad tattoos. A couple of similar unfortunates at the bar are smirking at this crude, but it must be granted accurate, appraisal of Marianna's sexual desirability.

"She's Old Bill mate. Just over here from Spain to learn about our anti-drug policies. My colleague and I are Home Office advisors to the drug squad. Idea is we show her around a bit. Real Rottweiler though; we were out last night in this boozer, some bloke skinned up in the corner, next thing she's on the phone to the cops and they're down there mob handed. Pulled the bloke and started searching everyone else. Real scene I can tell you."

"Fuckin' 'ell mate, bit unnecessary ain't it? Better stay well clear of that then, ain't we boys?"

35

A series of head nodding, sage glances, and affirmations of "fucking too right Gal" ensue, before I grab the drinks and take my leave to a chorus of "nice one" and "see you later mate".

"Do you know those guys Harry? They look very nasty. They're not going to come over here are they?"

Marianna's asking this but Douglas is the one who's looking really concerned, squirming in his seat and trying to half look over his shoulder without catching their glance.

"Just asking if we fancied joining them for a drink, said we were OK on our own. They were pretty insistent, think they fancied you. It's OK though. I said Douglas was your boyfriend and he's very jealous. Hopefully they won't come over now, never know though. Guys like that sometimes won't take no for an answer. Still, we'll sort them out won't we Douglas? Or is it Dougie?"

"It's Douglas. Anyway, I'll probably not hang around; want to catch up with the others before they leave. Just have this and go."

"Seems a shame. I mean, I know Marianna's very keen to learn more about the consultancy, aren't you babes?"

Gal and his mates have been joined by a couple of other desperadoes and they keep looking over our way. Douglas has picked up on this and radiates the appearance of a man experiencing discomfort of an extreme nature.

"Look guys, I really think I'd better be making a move. Early start and all that, you know how it is. Nice to have met you Marianna; you've got my card."

And with that he's gone, the lime still in place in the neck of his beer. Marianna looks a little concerned.

"Should we go with him, maybe take him somewhere else?"

"No he's fine, we'll finish our drinks then go somewhere else, just the two of us."

But judging by the look on her face, she's not a happy bunny.

"Harry, you shit, why did you bring us to this place? It's so horrible. You knew I wanted to talk to that guy about the consultancy but you just wanted to get rid of him so you could try to fuck me. I hate you sometimes."

She's getting up to go and I think she's close to tears, fuck me this is all going pear shaped.

"Come on Marianna, you know that's not true. I didn't ask the guy to leave. Anyway, he was a boring bastard. Look, let's go somewhere for dinner. I even promise I won't try to hit on you, OK?"

"No, it's not OK. This course is serious for me Harry. You think everything is a joke but it's not. I spent all my savings to come here. Do you know how many years it takes in Mexico to earn enough money to pay for this? My family are not rich; I have loans to pay back afterwards. I need to get a good job to make this all worthwhile. It is different for you. It's impossible for you to understand how difficult it is for me to be taken seriously as a woman back home. That's why this is all so important to me."

"OK, sure I understand what you're saying. But fuck me you can do better than consultancy. You really want to spend sixty hours a week pounding on Powerpoint, just to make a few partners rich? I've told you: go into the City, you're perfect for it."

"You're so full of shit, Harry! If it's so that you're such a big man in the City, why are you here then? You were sacked, no?"

Her eyes are still flashing angrily but she looks like she regrets saying this. I just shake my head and knock back my beer. She gets up to leave, I put my arm on hers but she shakes it off angrily and walks out. At the door she stops and looks over and shakes her head slowly. I realise then that I'm never going to know what it's like to make love to her. Think about going after her and apologising, trying to salvage our friendship. Reckon her struggles with finance and accounting will ensure that though, so instead I finish my drink and leave this scene of the doomed calling Theresa on the way. Never does to be without a fallback option.

"Harry, where have you been? I've been trying to call you all evening, I thought we were meant to be going out."

"I've just been a bit busy, but forget about that - I'm free now. Be over in ten minutes."

Turns out she's in her union bar with her mates. Fucked if I'm in the mood for that dingy shithole.

"Sweetheart, I've had a long day. Let's just go back to your place. I'll grab a bottle of wine on my way over."

"Oh OK, but you...you will stay for a while this time won't you, Harry?"

"Yeah, of course. Look I really want to see you Theresa, just been a bit tied up recently, that's all."

Pick up a bottle of some South American plonk from the supermarket. Make sure it's 14% alcohol so a couple of glasses will get her nice and warmed up. It's starting to rain so get a taxi over there. She's waiting for me outside. Looks like she's just changed as there's a pair of jeans and a jumper lying on the single bed. The little blue A-line mini-skirt, tight white top and leather boots she's changed into is certainly an improvement and I'm suddenly glad I came. Her make-up looks like it's been freshly, if rather hastily, applied as well.

"Harry, angel, I've missed you. When you didn't call I thought maybe you didn't want to see me any more. I thought maybe you'd found someone else."

She's looking up at me all wide-eyed, hoping that I'll reassure her how groundless her fears are.

"Theresa, c'mon babe. You know how I feel about you. Every chance I get I'm over here. I mean, just look at you. Any guy who didn't appreciate you'd be an idiot. Now, come on, let's get inside, have a drink and relax."

Once we're in her bedroom I'm opening the wine, telling her to get a couple of glasses. She reaches up to a shelf above her sink to get them and her skirt rides all the way to the bottom curve of her ass. She looks behind her and catches me staring.

"Do you still think I'm pretty, Harry?"

I set the bottle down and walk over behind her, putting my hand on her thigh and running it up inside her skirt. She's looking quite flushed now and I realise she's had a few to drink already, probably don't even need the wine.

"Bet all those young guys are lusting after you down at the union bar, eh?"

"Just one or two." She shrugs as she says it.

"Sure you wouldn't rather be with one of them?"

"No Harry, I only want you."

She's pouting when she says this and I'm well up for it now, my jeans and boxer shorts round my ankles as I pull her top off over her head. She's not wearing a bra and my left hand finds its way to her firm smooth breasts where they stay while I struggle to slip on a condom with my free hand, after opening it with my teeth. Theresa's unhooked her skirt and pulled her knickers down and is looking at herself in the mirror, pushing her chest out and running one hand through her hair while the other grips the sink. I'm in her and she's bent over the sink but still looking in the mirror as I'm taking her from behind. She's mouthing something as she smiles at me, urging me on wordlessly. I'm admiring Theresa admiring herself which gets me going big-time and I come quickly, leaving her looking a bit disappointed.

"It's OK Harry, really. I don't mind when that happens. It doesn't matter. Just stay the night, then we can do it again later, can't we?"

She leans back into me, putting an arm back behind her and around my neck. We stagger back and fall on her bed. I land on top of a pair of wet denim jeans. She's holding tight to me, making it difficult to throw them off the bed. The sugary pop music that's been playing on her cheap stereo since I got here is seriously annoying now. Looking at Theresa, whose falling asleep with her mouth open, I feel a familiar need to get the fuck out of here. I subtly try to extricate myself from her limpit grip without waking her, but no chance.

"Harry, where are you going? You're not leaving already, are you?"

"Sorry Babe, I've got a class first thing I need to prepare for. Look, I'll call you tomorrow."

"Harry, you promised. Harry wait…"

But I'm out the door as the words trail off behind me. Smart move not even bothering to undress before doing the business. Reckon it's time to call a few of the lads. Could murder a pint and some civilised male company. As I walk out of the door of her block that cloying pop music is still ringing in my head.

Chapter Five

Balbeck Toyevski

This first term has been very hard for you, as you knew it would be. Having to study fourteen or fifteen hours at least every day, just to keep up. Remember this is not Bishkek, you cannot expect to come here and be top of the class. You know that, but still feel ashamed. Squirming in your seat, hoping that the professors do not pick you out in class to answer questions in case you appear foolish; thinking carefully what you want to say in study group; not wanting to disagree with the others even if you think they are wrong. But now the term is over and you are still here, so try not to be too concerned about the exams in January. Yes, people say that they are very difficult but work very hard and you will pass them. Just like you always do back home. You worry too much. This has always been your problem, screwing up your face in concentration all the time, giving people the wrong impression of you. It is good that the big group presentation today is over. How fortunate it was to have Simone in your group, she is so clever and always takes control.

It is natural to miss Tamara very much, and the family, and indeed many things in England are very different than in Bishkek. But be brave and make everyone proud of you. Just think of the prestige you will receive back home from having studied here, of the respect given to your younger brothers because of what you have achieved. You will be a respected man of education and travel. Remember when you came back home from being an exchange student in Russia and Germany? The look on Tamara's face when everyone would gather round in Bishkek to hear stories about going to a rock concert in Moscow or a football match in Munich. Sometimes you exaggerated your stories a little, but so what? Everyone at home will be even more interested to hear what it was like to study in England. At last, you and Tamara will be able to get married and start a family. It is important for our country that you succeed in your studies here in England. Maybe more Kyrgyz can then come here to study afterwards. Remember the faith the professors at the American University in Bishkek placed in you when they awarded the scholarship to come and study here? Take strength from that and repay that trust.

41

Tonight is the end of term party and it is right that you have decided to go. Life here is not all about books. It will be the first time you have gone to a party for many weeks. Tonight it is time to let people see you smile, not frown. Tonight should be a night to remember.

Simone Sanders

"He's consistently failing to hold the attention of the class, is ill-prepared and frankly, is wasting our time. It's simply not good enough."

I'm letting Hilary Jenkins-Spires have the air-time here; she just better make sure she uses it. We're in the course director's office. There's a situation here with one of the lecturers who just isn't cutting it. Too jumpy, can't communicate for shit, doesn't challenge people talking crap. Basic stuff they'd never get away with back home. Hilary's our class rep. Well, being a Brit she was always going to get voted in on home turf. I'm here riding shotgun - she shows any sign of cutting this loser any slack though and all bets are off. I mean, it's not like Hilary and I are in the same bitch circle or anything, just you gotta know who punches their weight and give them a little respect, for now anyway. The course director's not looking too happy at this little end of term intrusion. Tries to blank us with some crap about the guy being a talented research student with some heavy duty academic duty citations. Don't mean jack if he can't handle his shit in the classroom. Hilary's getting blindsided here.

"Professor, I think what Hilary's calling you on is we're customers here, not undergraduates. We set high standards for ourselves and expect those same standards from the faculty. As Course Director, we look to you to defend our interests and right now that means acknowledging there's an expectation gap with this member of faculty."

He leans back in his chair and holds out his palms in what's obviously intended as a conciliatory gesture.

"OK, you've both made your point very eloquently. What I suggest is that you take the opportunity afforded to you by the 360 degree assessment system we have in place here to record this very valuable feedback."

"And then?"

"I'm sorry Simone, I'm not following you?"

"Then he gets stripped of his teaching responsibilities I assume?"

Hilary looks a bit concerned at this. Typical spineless Brit, not prepared to tough this thing out. Course Director actually has the cheek to look offended, be a different story if it was his money that was being squandered.

"I'm afraid there's no question of that, Simone. This is someone's career we're dealing with here. Surely you don't want to be responsible for jeopardising that?"

"Of course we don't professor, the student body here are very appreciative and supportive of our academics. We simply feel a more consistent level of teaching quality would be appropriate, isn't that right Simone?"

Thanks, bitch.

"Indeed, my main concern in all this is for the weaker students in our class, those who most suffer from below par teaching. I think it's my duty to speak up for them, that's why I'm here with Hilary to-day."

"Yes, quite, I see. Well I'm glad we've had the opportunity here to-day to discuss your concerns and please rest assured my door is always open to discuss any such issues you may have. Although perhaps it would be helpful if you could make an appointment next time. Anyway, I hope to see you both at the dinner tonight."

He opens the door to usher us both out. Sure he slammed it shut a little harder than he needed to.

"Well, I thought that was productive. Broadly speaking I'd surmise that we achieved our objectives. We've clearly stated we expect them to raise the bar for teaching standards. I'll make sure the rest of the class are kept in the loop."

Bullshit, we got fobbed off with lame-ass excuses. Screw that lazy asshole's career, if he can't teach his subject what's he doing wasting my time and money? In the US, they'd sue, here they just shrug their shoulders and accept it, pathetic really. I say something non-committal and Hilary and I go our separate ways. It's always the same old shit with people like her, don't have the balls to achieve closure. Guess it's 'cause they don't have to. Everything's always set up on a plate for them. Never have to get down and dirty like the rest of us.

Go downstairs to the common room. There's a few people milling around but it's got that end of term feel, kinda anti-climatic, like the intensity's gone from the place. Take that away and this is just another building. That Balbeck guy from my study group is there, weird name or what? He's from that place I've never heard of, can't pronounce and have less than zero interest in ever visiting. I mean it's all well and good the faculty here making such a big deal of the diversity of our student body but what good does

43

it do me if that translates into a heap of charity funded losers from the third world? He's sitting on his own reading, looks up, sees me and smiles. Always looks real nervous, like he's carrying the weight of the world on his shoulders. Looks like he expects me to come over and hang out with him. Forget that, term's over and with it our casual acquaintance. This first term's been a real ball-breaker. Lot of fourteen hour days, the pressure's never let up, but that suits me, sorts out the winners from the wannabees. I haven't blown off a single lecture, have covered every bit of reading, even the stuff that's only recommended. Not just the academic stuff either. I've been elected chair of the MBA Women in Finance society. Well, I was the obvious choice really. Most of the rest of them had only ever worked in the public sector or some other kinda lame-ass shit. Managed to persuade this real high profile female fund manager to come up and talk to us. This chick's heavy duty, had a family and a career, published books and everything, guess what? Have to strong arm the lazy bitches to come along, even then it was a 50% no show and had to pad it out with some PhD's and undergrads. Well, it was either that or invite the guys which woulda kinda defeated the object of the exercise. So what that it was a 7:30am breakfast meeting, you got something better to do? I swear to you, some of these chicks need to get with the program. Couple of years in equity sales would soon sort their shit out. Drag their sorry asses like they do here and they'd soon find themselves out on the street.

We had a big study group presentation to-day; it went OK. I mean, I was a little disappointed in some of the others but what can you expect from them? I stayed up all last night overhauling the whole presentation, forced the rest of the group to accept the changes. It wasn't easy, one or two of them were pissed at me, it nearly turned into a major confrontation, but in the end I persuaded the majority it was the right option. I know some of them are relieved not to be working with me anymore but I'm not interested in being their friend. I just need to ensure they don't prevent me from achieving what I came here to do.

Anyway, tonight I can relax, hang out a little bit. We're all getting together, throwing a party. Time for me to be sociable, show my human face. I've been a little tense recently. Don't want people to think I'm not approachable. After all, I'm here to network as well. Have to make sure I'm talking to the right people though. These events have to be approached carefully, get stuck with the wrong people for too long and the evening's wasted. Maybe find out if there's anyone worth hanging out with here over the vacation. Of course I'm not going home for Christmas. Tipton sucks and I'm not quite ready to go back to San Francisco yet. Anyway, the exams are in January so I'll keep busy preparing for those. My grades have been good so far but these Brits are real tight-assed bastards when it comes to marking. No way am I going into those exams unprepared. My love life sucks as well. I've been too busy and there just aren't the men here. I mean British accents are sexy, well some of them, the ones I can understand, but the men are just not attractive. I mean like, come on. They're pale, got bad skin, don't work out enough and have you seen their teeth? The students that are OK, they're mostly taken or gay, like Olaf. I guess three years in the Finnish army does that to a guy. Bummer though - the times I've imagined getting off on that. As for the rest of them, if the British girls don't want them, what the fuck am I meant to do with them? So it's been pretty barren on that front. It's tough. I mean, what am I supposed to do, go out with some schmuck just to get laid? I am feeling pretty horny though. Terms over and it has been awhile. Some of the Latin guys are quite hot. I'll see how tonight plays out. I'm pretty beat having been up all night. Still got some of that coke left though. Shouldn't really, but it is end of term after all and I have been working so hard. In fact, I might just get a little more. Hey, I don't want to run out tonight do I? Though it means dealing with that slimeball, Billy. Maybe I'll find a way to report him when I've left. Serve him right, he's such a sleaze. Works in the kitchen at the business school. I'm sure he just uses it as a front to deal to the students from. He used to pop up in the pubs we drank in at the start of term, that's how I got in with him. Then, we were in a club one night and he was there. It was hot, loud and sweaty. I was dancing and at the same time looking around to see if anyone was dealing. He just came up behind me and asked me if I needed anything. Don't know why he approached me, not like I give of those vibes or anything, but hey I'm not complaining. Anyway, I better get ready. Tonight Simone is putting her party face on.

Danny McMullen

"OK guys, everyone agreed that's the de-brief concluded? Good, I think we've all learned from this experience as a group. Let's look to leverage that in our new study groups next term. Hope we get to work together again. Anyone got anything they'd like to add, Sarah, Winston, Chong, Danny, Nakata…?"

"Thank-you very much, Charles. So good of you for all your help to me this term."

The others nod at this comment from Nakata.

45

"It's been my pleasure, Nakata, and I've gained a great insight into Japanese business values and culture from you this term."

Everyone murmurs in agreement with this, she smiles and drops her head looking embarrassed and pleased at the same time. To be fair, reckon I'm gonna miss working with these dudes. They weren't so bad once we all stopped trying to size each other up and got on with trying to keep our shit together and get through this term. Couple of them even bailed my ass out when I was getting pulped in front of the class by that hot-shot overseas lecturer. Just my luck to get called on the morning after the Mark Gardener gig. Shit man, I'd only had about three hours sleep, what by the time we left the place and caught the last train home. Was way too stoked to sleep when I did get home, especially as I'd even managed to shake the main man's hand after the gig. Ended up having a smoke and playing his music most of the night, least 'til the dude in the next room starts banging my door, threatening to kick the shit out of me. Guess it musta been a bit louder than I thought. Just about made it in the next morning, thought about blowing it off but that's kinda lame. Wished I had though once I got there. I was just chilling at the back of the class reliving the events of the previous night when I hear my name being called. Think he'd called it twice before someone elbowed me in the ribs and nodded towards the front where the lecturer was standing with his arms folded, looking up at me with an expectant sneer. Could hear him drumming his fingers on the lectern as I clambered past people to get to the stairs leading down to the front.

"In your own time please, Mr. McMullen."

This drew smirks from several of the faces in the front row that were turned to watch me shuffling down the stairs.

Once I got down there this lecturer guy cut through my attempts at vague waffle, demanding I demonstrate appropriate experience curve strategies and potential alternative implementation scenarios.

"I need specific frameworks relating to the case here Mr. McMullen. What you're giving me are broad-based generalisations with no merit in addressing the key issues."

Might as well have asked me to perform open-heart surgery, just wasn't happening. Finally, he puts it to me that I hadn't prepared for the class at all, not a spectacularly difficult deduction I guess but humiliating all the same.

"Mr. McMullen, the level of analysis you're providing here is what I'd expect from a first year undergraduate, not an MBA candidate. Unless you can demonstrate you've given any genuine

46

thought to this case, there is little point in you continuing to waste the classes' time."

Am just standing there taking this guy's shit when Charles steps in and says that actually I'd had an important personal commitment the night before and we'd all agreed as a study group that I'd sit this one out. Course the man at the front isn't too impressed by this and starts in on Charles who unlike me gives as good as he gets, pointing out that rigid approaches to the division of labour have no place in modern management thinking. Must have been my lucky day 'cause this gets me out of jail, and I haul my sorry ass back to my seat thinking, not for the first time, that whatever I'm cut out for in life it sure as hell isn't this.

Just as I'm getting all nostalgic someone asks if we're all going to the end of term dinner tonight. Everyone else says they are. I don't say anything, unfortunately this doesn't go unnoticed and before I know it two or three of them are cajoling me into it. That's the thing about this place, people are so damned enthusiastic. As usual I take the path of least resistance: sure man why not? Some of them split for a drink now, I decide against it, this has been a long day. Ended up having a late one last night over at Miguel's. He'd bought the DVD version of Once Upon a Time in the West. Three hours long man, but it would've been a crime not to watch it. Was gone 1am before I was in bed. Had to be here by 8am to prepare for our study group presentation at three o'clock. Am I ever glad that's over. I guess it went OK. I could've contributed a bit more, but I did what I was asked to do. People like Charles just like to run the gig and that's fine by me. I'm a bit older than some of them anyway. I guess they're just real young and keen, basically more ambitious than I am. That's been the tough thing about being here. Not the work; some of it's harder than others but that doesn't bother me. I actually don't mind studying, never have. Guess that's why I ended up staying on and starting the PhD in Urban Migration at Queens back home in Ontario. Shame I never ended up finishing it but I met Karen when I was over here at UCL for a year and she really wanted us to stay in England. Then Caitlin was born and no way was Karen moving half way round the world with a baby. Thought I could maybe get a position lecturing but there wasn't much doing, so I ended up working in local government town planning. Guess it kinda uses what I studied, well a little anyway, and it's an easy gig to be honest, and the money's just about enough to live on. Most of it goes to Karen for Caitlin anyway. I dig living in London. It's a cool city. I like the anonymity; easy to just melt into the background. I'm not really one for being the centre of attention, that's why I find these group presentations such a drag. I thought

47

maybe the MBA would make me more self-confident, better able to handle those type of situations, but it hasn't. In fact, probably the opposite. Most people here exude confidence. Still, term's over and I got through it OK. Now I can think about the vacation. Obviously I'm staying here, have rented my flat out in London and don't really have the cash to go back to Canada. Still remember the look on my mother's face last Christmas when I pitched up without Caitlin. For an instant there was genuine warmth in her smile, but then even though she knew I was coming alone, her eyes looked for a four-year-old granddaughter who wasn't there. My dad just shook my hand quickly then put his arm round my mother and led us through the airport in near silence. Even on Christmas Day when my three sisters all had their kids over it still felt like I'd let them down. At least I'll be able to spend a bit of time with Caitlin over the break. Haven't seen that much of her since I started here. Course I gotta keep sending the checks to Karen, but the work pressures been too great. What with the time it takes to travel up to Manchester where they live now and all that. I'm hoping to get up there this weekend, maybe bring her down here for a few days next week, just before Christmas, when she gets out of school. Give me the chance to do the kinda things with her that Dads are meant to do. Go to the movies, buy her pizza, just simple stuff, but it cuts me in half when I can't do it. I'll have to stay off the weed then too. Don't want her to see me stoned. Plenty of time for that after she's gone.

I guess I should go to this party tonight. Not really my scene, black-tie and all that but hey people seemed to want me to go and like I said earlier these dudes are kinda ok really. Maybe Simone'll be there. Haven't really spoken to her since that afternoon a couple of months ago when Harry and I helped dump her stuff. Keep thinking about her though. Haven't really had much luck with women since Karen and I split up. I mean, I've dated a couple of people from work but it just hasn't felt right, y'know? Not that there's been anything wrong with these chicks I've dated, just seemed kinda pointless spending time with them. Simone though, now that could be a whole other matter. Probably out of my league but you never know 'til you try.

Harry Stanton

" I want the smartest car you've got. Make sure you stick a couple of chilled bottles of Veuve Clicqout in the mini-bar as well. Be ready to pick me up about half-seven, I'll let you know where from."

"OK boss, no sweat. There's a new driver on tonight, Rio. He'll be taking care of things, that fine by you?"

"Sweet, doesn't matter who drives. Just stick it on my tab. Stanton, Harry Stanton."

Term's over and school's out. Presentation successfully completed with leading role for yours truly, of course. Now Harry boy is ready to party. Tonight's the class do, could this be the chance to cash in my chips for all those hours of help I gave the lovely Marianna in her struggles with the complexities of derivatives pricing? Talking about cashing in chips, I mustn't forget the even lovelier but highly elusive Simone, who I rescued in her hour of distress and of whom I have seen little since, although her reputation, it has to be said, does proceed her. Think you're able to coast through a presentation with her in the audience, think again. Mind you, the sight of her kicking shit out of some muppet who just didn't have their shit together is pretty fucking erotic in a twisted way. It's this desire for carnal knowledge of my two classmates that's ensured a careful plan has been laid out for tonight. A few of us livelier lads are meeting up early doors to imbibe a little champagne before arriving at the pre-dinner cocktails. Doesn't do to arrive too early to these things of course. Leave that to the socially inept amongst us, of which I am afraid to say there are rather a few. After the dinner I have hired a limousine to ferry a couple of us down to one of the members clubs I frequent in London. I've left a couple of vacant places for the fittest amongst the young ladies on the course, of which naturally pride of place will be reserved for Simone and Marianna. A ménage a tres would, it must be said, be the ideal way to end the term, but I fear that may prove a little ambitious even for me. I'm confident that faced with the truly appalling alternatives offered here by way of late night entertainment, I should have little problem persuading them to accompany us. As a back-up Theresa and a couple of the female hunting fraternity will I am certain be delighted to abandon whatever undergraduate dive they find themselves in and accompany my merry band. The whole evening has been meticulously planned, nothing left to chance. What could possibly go wrong?

Chapter Six

Simone Sanders

Need to get that goddamn caretaker over here to fix this leaking tap. Charge enough for this shitty shoebox, least they could do is service the place. Not as if they even furnish it properly. All cheap and nasty stuff. The sofa's got all kinda stains on it, disgusting. Least I know the mattress is new, made them produce the receipt for it. Otherwise would've probably ended up sleeping on someone else's spunk stains, gross. Still, suits my purposes here. Like I was ever gonna go back to living in a student dorm full of juiced up kids. Does make me yearn for the apartment I used to have in San Fran though. Prime Bay Area real estate that was, all the social prestige you could've asked for in a zip code. Course I wasn't paying for it, no way. I mean what else was Hamilton there for? I mean the guy was a real lame-ass but he was making the bucks. Sure, he'd like to have been a player but he was just too Mid-Western for that. The product of good solid Kansas City stock. Still knew the value of a dollar. I put it down to the fact his family actually cared about their reputation, bought into that civic pride bullshit. His grandfather had been on the board of a couple of corporations but never plundered them. Not the way an Ivy League, East Coaster woulda done. Those values musta got distilled through the genes. Even made it clear when he asked me out that him being a major client shouldn't affect my decision one iota. Bummer he figured it out about Patrick but state I was in, even Hamilton was bound to notice something was up. Hamilton and I'd been together three years and I'd been seeing Patrick for almost half that time. Reckon I'd still be getting away with it too, if I hadn't gotten pregnant. When Hamilton did finally get the picture even that didn't get him pissed. Just said he felt beat up. That he'd always tried to see the best in me. Splitting up meant having to drag my sorry ass back to my parents for six months. Boy, I tell you I was going out clean out of my mind with boredom there. Least it made me get my shit together and get accepted for this place pronto. Exactly what else was I supposed to do? Join Future Farmers of America and knit patchwork peace quilts? Start looking up old school friends like my mom suggested? I mean come on!

Now and again I'd bump into them in the street, literally in some cases given the damn size of them.

"Oh my goodness, just look at you! You haven't gained an ounce since High School. Wish I could say the same but that's what three kids does for you."

We're standing in the doorway of the drugstore and I just can't get past her.

"Your Mom says you're off to England to study. Gee, that sounds real neat. You make sure and give my regards to the Queen if you meet her. Tell her Tipton says 'Hi!'"

Only popped in to pick up some prescription sleeping pills but looks like I'm stuck here reliving junior high with lardass. Try stepping back into the store to let her through but nope, she just carries on telling me about her florist business, "Blossoming Buds, proud to be a Christian business", in the loudest goddamn voice I've ever heard. Get to that size you'd think you'd whisper rather than bellow. Finally, a car horn starts tooting, non-stop.

"That'll be Marshall, my youngest. Only two but so smart for his age. It's OK sweetie, Mommy's coming. Guess I better pick up their Ritalin and run. You be sure and stop by the store before you leave for England now. We'll be praying for you all the way over there."

She waddles up to the counter freeing the doorway which I bolt out of and into my Mom's station wagon. Reversing onto the high street I see she's still in there yacking away at the counter while a red-faced Marshall pounds the window and beeps the horn in the SUV parked next to me, an empty candy wrapper clenched in his pudgy fist. Least bumping into me'll give her something to brag about at her next coffee morning. Suppose it must be painful to see what I've achieved in my life and compare it to her own.

As if just living in that goddam town wasn't enough of a drag, I also had to deal with my parents' getting on my case, suggesting I see a counsellor. Well that was just plain dumb. Naturally I had one in San Francisco, well I'd been through several actually, but who the fuck was gonna be smart enough to interact with me in Hicksville Tipton? Of course there were no suitable job openings for me there either. Get real. Nope, I just worked out like crazy there to keep my ass in shape, went through all the pre-reading for this course and put up with the social vacuum I found myself in. Got myself a little lovin' from Travis, a personal trainer from the gym, but then he starts trying to take it to another level. Dude, just be grateful for what it is, sooo tedious when that happens. Such a waste too, great pecs. Thankfully I've enough cash stashed away from San Francisco to get me through the year here without slumming it too bad. Real advantage of a one-year programme, I tell you. That's one thing we just haven't cottoned on to back home yet. Why spend twice as long doing the same thing? The pay-off Patrick helped negotiate on my behalf helped of course. Well over the odds, considering I quit, but so what? I'd more than earned it, amount of business I pulled in for that firm over the years. Secret in selling to these hedge fund manager assholes is to pretend you know they're smarter than you are. I mean we're in one of the shittiest bear markets in history and these guys think they deserve the Nobel Prize 'cause they make money outta shorting stock, gimme a fucking break. Guys like that, and don't listen to any feminist bullshit 'cause nine out of ten are guys, buy from girls like me. Whether I'm selling stock or table dancing, no matter, just remember they're the ones who didn't get laid enough at college, now they're calling the shots they're an easy mark. I don't mean I had to sleep with them or anything, just push the right buttons and the commission came tumbling in. When I go back though I'm on the other end of the telephone. Make some real bucks of my own.

So here I am, almost ready to go. Taxi should be here any minute, just have a little something to set me up and then I'll be all fine and dandy. Pop into the bathroom, chop a little out, get my little silver spoon out, three month anniversary present from Patrick. Hope that sonofabitch of a dealer hasn't ripped me off. There we go, instant nirvana. Just do the other nostril, fuck there's the phone, just let it go to answer-phone, probably just my mom bitching about my not coming home for Christmas.

"Simone, hi, this is a message from Trent Ledbetter of Ledbetter Capital. Simone I just wanted to say…"

Fuck I better take this call, snort the other spoonful real quick and get to the phone.

"…thanks for your resume which we received and I assure you we'll be …."

"Trent, Hi, Simone Sanders here. Trent, I'm going out to dinner in five minutes so let's nail it down. What can Ledbetter Capital offer me? I'm fielding a lot of calls, Trent, shoot."

"Uh right, OK, what I was actually gonna say Simone is… well it was a courtesy call really to thank-you for your resume and we might be interested in talking with you when you graduate, but unfortunately we haven't got any vacancies right now and well to be honest we usually recruit out of the two year programs over here so …"

"OK Trent, I'm going to put it to you that any dumb-ass can take two years out of their lives and putz around drinking cocktails. It takes a high altitude player to step up to the plate and nail it

53

down in a year. Let's stop wasting time here Trent, are we talking or not?"

"Well, actually for the record I'm Wharton class of '96 myself, basically thank-you for your resume but we don't recruit out of one year programmes from mid-table schools."

"You phoned to tell me that? Who the fuck are you? The office manager or some dumb-ass in HR? Do you know how sought after I am?"

"Actually lady, I'm the managing partner and I don't know what your problem is but I suggest you get it sorted and quick."

Then the asshole hangs up on me, probably some crankcaller… feel bit unsteady, remember haven't eaten, momentarily nauseous, soon passes, fuck it that asshole's brought me back down. Better do a little more, work my ass of all term then some dumb-ass tries to rain on my parade. That's better, screw him anyway, probably some nerd that hasn't been laid in a year. Look in the mirror, I'm a sexy bitch, where's the taxi, need to get there now, pace the floor, check my phone, no messages, why's taxi late, feeling horny, need to get laid, want Travis' cock, how fucking smart am I? Fuck Ledbetter Capital, what kinda asshole names their firm after themself? Buddy, take some of that cash you're raking in and go buy yourself an imagination. Who cares though? Not me, I'm a Money Honey, everyone knows that, teeth are numb, need a drink, champagne, no vodka martini, no champagne, can't make vodka martini here, good coke, better than in Tipton, feel nauseous again, retch, haven't eaten, not hungry, how much have I got left, enough, I hope. Have dealer's number, scumbag, all men are, fucking asshole Patrick, I'm in control though. Where's taxi, taxi's here, halleluiah, kiss Nicholas' photo, did mom think I'd forget, off to party, feeling fucking sexy, these people are lucky to know me, climb in back seat, let's get there fast, then find a bathroom. Have I enough, better call dealer, can't be caught short, no answer, fuck, should have enough, turn the music up please, teeth no longer numb, turn music down will you, try dealer again, leave message, stuck in traffic, goddam roundabouts, what's wrong with this country. We're close, hurry up, arrive, pay driver, make entrance, all eyes on me, find bathroom, out of my way bitch, empty cubicle, that's better, retch again, that's better, teeth numb again, I'm flying. Hi there sweetie, you look great, suits you well, hi hardly recognised you, boy don't you clean up well, I know, such a relief to have it over, decided to stay here actually, there's the Dean, say Hi, shake hands, enjoying rising to the challenge Dean, absolutely, loving it, the pace is simply exhilarating, exploring number of options at present, alternative investments has definite potential, I agree, essential to maintain career momentum. Slug down champagne, need more, dumb-ass waiter, grab another, retch again, Dean talking to me, absolutely, feeling fine, champagne went down wrong way, not used to it, don't drink really you see, just thought I'd be sociable tonight. Phone rings, excuse me Dean, need to take this, probably a headhunter from the States.

"Hey Billy, you've called back, thank God. I just need a little something again, it's the holidays now and I'm in the mood to party a little. Help me out like now, OK?"

"Tomorrow, are you fucking kidding me, what do you mean you're off to London with a mate tonight? ....Sorry Billy, you know I don't mean to get pissy with you, it's just I really need it right now. Come on, I'm your best customer. Listen, I'm at this stupid Christmas party, just get it over to me now and I'll pay a little more. Please Billy, you know I'm good for the money, be a darling."

"Thanks Billy, I'm like so grateful, OK, you'll be here soon, right? Sure, sure, that's cool, just call me soon as you get here."

Get back inside, just keep that asshole sweet tonight, give up tomorrow. Another glass of champagne, why didn't Patrick leave her, I'm much younger, prettier, smarter, fuck him, it was our baby, people going into dinner, not hungry, go to bathroom again, check supplies, running low, need dealer soon, have another line, that's better, retch, teeth numb, so who am I sitting beside, check seating plan, who the fuck's she, sounds Chinese, shit he's boring and ugly, oh my God anyone but him. I should be on the fucking A-table, beside the Dean, must have been a mistake, someone needs to get their shit together. Spot Harry, place beside him's free still, swap name settings, Hi honey, so good to see you, me, yeah been real busy, hoped we catch up tonight, absolutely fine, really looking forward to letting my hair down tonight, been working so hard, you look good, been working out, what am I doing later on, London, love to come with you, sounds real cool, can't wait, where's the champagne, and you are, thanks that's so sweet of you, that's my phone, need to take this call, back in a moment, so good to catch up with you. Damn, it's hard work being so popular.

Harry Stanton

"So this fella's buck naked with a hard on in full view of two hundred chest-beating Neanderthals. Fuckin' sketch I tell you."

We're in what passes for a classy bar in this town having a little pre-dinner sharpener. Big Sean's regaling us with this anecdote about being at a sales conference when he worked for one of the big life assurance companies. Apparently they used to take all the top producers away to Mexico or somewhere else exotic. Let them piss it up big style for a couple days, shag the local hookers and generally make merry. Anyway, on the pretence there was a purpose to the trip they used to make them sit through training sessions for a couple of hours in the morning, before they went on the rampage. Which is why Sean's there lecturing on compliance, which as I'm sure you can imagine they had about as much interest in as a lecture on safe sex. He's mid-flow about new FSA regulations on know your customer, blah-de-blah when they all start laughing, then standing up and cheering at something obviously going on through the glass wall behind him. Sean turns around and one of the salesmen is backstroking naked up the middle of the swimming pool with a hard-on.

"OK, management skills session, you're all in my shoes. How do you deal with this little situation?"

George is straight in.

"Was the dude hung?"

"Built like a fucking skyscraper mate."

"Awesome, then it's class dismissed and I'm in there with him! God that's my fantasy a swimming pool full of naked insurance salesmen, they recruiting honey?"

Everyone's cracking up at this, someone else suggests Sean introduces it as a class discussion next term. Someone else asks how he did handle it.

"Pulled the blinds mate, simple solution's usually the right one."

Good answer, gets a deserved round of applause. Got to give it to the big man he knows how to get everyone in the party mood. Good turn-out tonight of those who matter. Couple of the other British lads, Big Sean from Belfast whose just regaled us with this choice anecdote, couple of the Canadians, and Pablo and Diego representing the Latin American contingent. Khalfan from Oman shows up as well, always useful as he's not shy about stumping up for the Dom Perignon, whereas the rest of us are on more of a Lanson Black Label budget. He's up at the bar now, credit card in hand, with George from New York, our token poof, top lad though, never anything less than immaculately turned out and a real gent. Anyway, as ever it's a good showing of the MBA's makers and shakers, no social inadequates need apply. We'd been getting together from mid-way through the first term, you know how it is. At first everyone hangs with everyone else, then people gravitate towards their own peer group. Find their own level so to speak and that's how it was with us. Formed our own little dining club too, invitation only of course, I mean this place is so politically correct most of the time. I don't have problem with that but sometimes boys just want to be boys you know what I mean? Our little soirees offered an opportunity to do just that. We're not talking wholesale debauchery, just decent dinner, fine drop of wine, brandy, cigars and cards, couple of trips to London for a visit to the casino followed by a spot of lap-dancing. All organised by yours truly of course, all very harmless and essential preparation for our corporate careers to follow. Sight more useful than Management Practice. Just a bit of male bonding, goes on all over the world, why should business school be any different? Let's face it, we're motivated by money, status, sex, same as the next man really. They can hang any label they want on it, but people stump up good money to come to a business school like this for the social prestige it offers, pure and simple, and our little club was just taking that a step further. If we don't ask you to join, don't take it too personally, we are after all highly selective. Entrance criteria include at least two of the following, money, charisma, connections, brains or just plain old self-confidence. Oh, and we all knew the score, what goes on tour stays on tour. So you want to get a few extras from the lapdancer? None of my business. Want to score a little Bolivian marching powder? Don't touch it myself but you go right ahead. We're all men of the world, after all. That's an essential qualification for membership: discretion, or put bluntly, knowing how to keep your mouth shut. Comes in handy in the real life business world too.

Time to drink up and go to the dinner. The Latin lads have got phone numbers from a couple of local ladies hanging round the bar, not exactly top drawer but definitely doable. Of course they've got long-term girlfriends back home, but hey, boys will be boys, right? After dragging them away from their, it has to be said, willing, conquests, we head over to the dinner in the stretch limo I've specially commandeered for the evening. Only a five minute drive, so get the guy to do a loop round the city centre, keeps the momentum going, then make sure the driver parks right up front by the door so everyone gets a good look at us. Tell the driver I'll see him in a couple of hours, make sure the mini-bars well stocked and don't be fucking late. In we go, with me leading the way of course and making a beeline straight for the champagne. It's drinkable, just about the cheapest they could reasonably get away with; Piper Heidseck I reckon. Tempted to order a bottle of Dom just to large it but tonight's already costing a fortune and anyway be rude to decline their almost generous hospitality wouldn't it? Stop for a minute and look around me. People are all clustered in little groups, there's a pattern to them, one person's holding court, usually someone a bit higher up the evolutionary ladder and the rest are kind of huddled around them, basking in their reflected glory. Course this suits the A-lister; they get to schmooze five or six people at once without really having to speak to any of them. Realise I don't really know anything meaningful about most of these people. This whole MBA thing is a strangely artificial environment, we spend all this time together behaving as though this is one of our central life experiences, but it isn't, it's just another year. Truth is, I believe you're either going to make it in this world or you aren't. This type of thing doesn't make one iota of difference. Read about this professor in the States once, Stanford or some other production line for go-getters, anyway this guy reckoned if you took half the class and just let them large it for England for two years and made the other half work, then awarded them both the degree, it would have no discernable impact on how they got on back in the real world. With you all the way there, mate. Reckon I'm living proof your little theory's correct, or at least I will be when I leave here. Still, don't want to get too philosophical on a night like tonight. Help myself to another glass of champagne and do the whole circulating bit. Now, where are the ladies?

Danny McMullen

Realise after I've agreed to go to this that I don't even own a tux. Costs fifty quid just to hire one. Wasn't even gonna go but it's end of term and all that so I suppose I should make the effort, 'specially as I expect Simone'll be there. Manage to get to the dress hire store in time. Lucky they got one off the peg that's a reasonable fit. Dude I feel stupid in these things, just don't seem to sit right on my body. Get home, there's a message on the answer-machine.

"Danny, it's Karen, guess you're not in. Anyway, just checking you're still coming up this Saturday to see Caitlin. She's really looking forward to it. Don't let her down Danny, she's only five years old. Oh, and by the way, I'm going out Saturday evening with Trevor so I'm relying on you to look after Caitlin, bye."

Make me feel like a worthless piece of shit, why don't you Karen? I never let my daughter down, you're the one who took her two hundred miles away from me. Shit, I was in a good mood before I got that message. Like I care that you're going out with Trevor and he gets to see more of my daughter than I do. It's like when we split up, or more accurately when she bailed on me, it was all my fault according to her. I wasn't prepared to take any initiative, was

58

too passive, she needed more from life, all that crap. Real truth is once Caitlin was born she just wanted to get back up to her family in Manchester. I was just in the way. Anyway man, forget it, life's too short. Feeling a bit beat so decide to have a lie down. Drift off to sleep and when I wake up it's already seven o'clock. Jesus the damn pre-dinner reception starts at seven-thirty, better get my ass into gear. Stick on some livelier 'gaze, Lovehappy by the charlottes. Feel pumped up by their tone of youthful insolence. Fuck Karen anyway, I'm going out tonight. Shower, dress, shit man can't tie this damn thing, knew I shoulda got a pre-tied one. Now I'm sweating so much trying to get the damn thing on my shirt's sticking to my back. I guess that'll do. Drink a cold beer, skin-up a quick spliff then head out. It's about a fifteen minute walk, shouldn't be too late, no big deal if I am though. Feeling a bit more relaxed now, kinda looking forward to tonight. Even more than that I'm looking forward to seeing Caitlin this weekend. Makes me smile and wince at the same time when I remember what she said last time we were together.

"Daddy, you're too old to be at school. Are you a teacher?"

"No sweetheart. Daddy's at a special school for big grown-up people, just for a year."

"What do they teach at grown-up school, Daddy? Do they teach you how to help sick people?"

"No sweetheart, that's what a doctor learns."

"So what do they teach then, Daddy? I want to know."

Realised she was getting impatient now so I better think of something. Well let's see now, they teach how to bullshit, self-promote and back-slap. Nope, not what a five-year-old wants to hear.

"They teach Daddy how to do lots of important things that rich business people do."

She looks doubtful at this.

"But Daddy, if you're rich can I have a pony?"

"What do you think you're playing at Danny? No you can't have a pony sweetheart, Daddy's just being silly. You know we don't have the space to keep one."

Karen's just looking at me and shaking her head now, having just came into the room as I was saying good-bye to Caitlin. Of course she's not gonna bother getting the full picture, just take what she heard and use it to portray me in a shitty light. I hate arguing in front of Caitlin so I drop it. Say my goodbyes and just go. Just because Karen and I have screwed up what we once had doesn't mean I lose my daughter as well, no way.

Get outside and start shivering in the cold. I should take a cab but money's tight. The scholarship only goes so far and I want to get Caitlin something cool for Christmas. No idea what yet, figure better have a look round the shops tomorrow, try and get some ideas. Walk quickly to try and keep warm, pull my coat tight around me, should've brought a scarf and gloves but was in a rush. Wonder what tonight'll be like. Not used to these dinner jacket kinda gigs, more of a jeans and sneakers guy, but they really dig them here. Gotta show willing I guess, although like Miguel said I do find myself asking what I'm doing here. Not exactly like I'm some kinda high achiever, is it? No doubt they'd probably say it's to get diversity of student body or some shit like that. Whatever man, I'm here now. Real fancy place too, one of these huge liveried halls with portraits of real serious looking old dudes on the panelled walls and waiters in white jackets. People are still drinking at the reception, haven't gone in for dinner yet, that's cool. Grab a glass of champagne and down it, tastes good, then another. Hey, maybe I could get used to this lifestyle after all. I mean I've gotta be on this course for a reason right? There's Simone, she's looking hot tonight. Go over to talk to her but she runs past me like she's in a hurry, goes outside to use her phone, then comes back in and heads straight to the bathroom. They're calling people into dinner, guess I'll catch up with her later. She looks a bit wired to be honest and it's still early. Fuck it, that's her business. Grab another glass of champagne before heading in to dinner. It's about time I loosened up a bit really.

Balbeck Toyevski

You are excited for the party tonight. This is a chance to learn more about your fellow students and maybe tell them more about Kyrgyzstan. How smart you look in the dinner suit you borrowed from your friend Arri. It is lucky that he is a similar size to you, although a little taller, and that he does not need his tonight. It is good to have such fine friends. It is time to make more peoples' acquaintance on the course. That is one of the reasons you are here after all. It is very different to Bishkek. There you knew everybody and were often involved in organising the social events, but here you must be more careful. Never forget it is a great honour to study at such a famous university with such clever students. Tonight, though, it is time to celebrate because the first term is over. Yes, of course you must study very hard to pass the exams next month, but it is right to begin to feel more confident that you will succeed

60

in getting awarded the MBA. It has been very difficult to find any time to relax since coming to the UK. Sometimes friends from home who are now living in London have asked you to come to visit, but you are always too busy studying. Anyway, you did not come to UK to meet other Kyrgyz. That you could have done at home in Bishkek. But tonight have some fun, bring out the Krygyz vodka you brought to the UK, maybe drink a little before the dinner. You will be more relaxed and able to talk freely with fellow students. Be careful though, sometimes in Bishkek you drank too much. Remember Tamara made you promise that would not happen here. Do not appear to be a drunkard in front of your classmates, this would bring great embarrassment. Oh how you wish that Tamara and the family and your friends could see how smart you look. Yes, have another glass of vodka before you go. You have been playing some pop music on the little stereo that was a leaving present from Tamara and your brothers. Suddenly you feel the need to hear some Kyrgyz music, even though back in Bishkek you always mocked it, preferring Western groups. The morning you left, Mother gave you a CD of her favourite traditional tunes. She had wrapped it up in silver paper and told you to listen to it if you ever felt homesick. You play it loudly, listening to the flutes and the komuz making the rousing sounds handed down over generations of nomads, reminding you of the snow-capped peaks and rushing brooks of home. It is time to be proud of who you are and what you have accomplished, not always be worried about what other people think. Why should anyone look down on you? You will just have one more vodka and listen to Mother's CD again. Leave after this though as the reception starts at 7:30pm and you should not be late as that would be rude. It is a short walk to the dinner, you may be early. On the way, you pass several English pubs. Maybe you will stop and try a glass of beer before the dinner. Here is one, it looks quite busy but look at the bar there are some classmates. This is your chance, go over to them, don't worry that they do not know you very well. They acknowledge you and someone gives you a beer. It is a large glass and the beer is cold and it tastes good. They are all laughing and joking with each other and one of them thumps you on the shoulder when he has finished telling a story. It is obvious they are pleased to see you. What were you worrying for? Someone is admiring your shoes and pointing them out to the others. A gift from Uncle, made specially for you by the best shoe-maker in Bishkek. He told you to save them for a special occasion and tonight is the first time you have worn them. Even though they hurt your feet you are proud that the others are admiring them. Drink the beer quickly and then buy another one for everyone as it seems this is the correct thing to do in England. Everyone is very relaxed and happy and there is time for one more beer before going to dinner. The beer is very easy to drink although it is a little gassy and makes you belch. Now the guy who was thumping you on the shoulder is slapping you on the back and has put a small glass of liquor in your hand which he says you must drink "down in one mate". Everyone starts to sing your name, "Balbeck, Balbeck!" as you drink it, then they all cheer. You check your watch as the dinner is meant to have started by now, but no one seems worried that they will be late. Someone tells you it is not expected that people arrive on time for a dinner in the UK, instead it is customary to stop and have several drinks in the pub first. This is useful information and after leaving the pub on the walk to dinner you tell them some stories about life in Kyrgyzstan. They must find these funny as they laugh a lot and encourage you to tell more. Now do you see that this was the right thing to do, to stop hiding away from everyone? Are you happy when you arrive at the dinner, with all your friends and classmates? If only people in Bishkek could see you now. Such great stories you will have to tell everyone when you go back home.

Chapter Seven

Harry Stanton

Fuck me I've landed at a bottom quartile table here and no mistake. Neil on my right can bore for England. Chick on my left I don't know, she's not there yet but name card sounds Japanese and a German opposite. Enough said. Thank God for Stelios who's also sitting opposite. Greek lad, likes his vino and his footie, should just about get me through the next two hours. Who the fuck elected that stupid Sarah cow from Glasgow social secretary? Just because she'd been here as an undergrad, trust her to fuck up my evening with this ridiculous seating plan. Should've just let us sit where we want, let the market decide and all that. That's the problem with people who get themselves elected to these kind of positions, they think it actually entitles them to make some decisions. Bollocks to that, they're just even more self-important than the rest of us. You can always tell them, they're the ones trying to hang out with the faculty, working the room, spending three minutes twenty seconds with everyone. Worked with people like that in the City too, always the ones who end up needing their ass wiped. Finish my champagne and look around for a waiter realising they're in short supply. Am considering slipping one of them a twenty spot to keep the wine flowing when I'm vaguely aware that there's a conversation going on around me.

"Your input would be invaluable Harry. You'd be able to bring the real-life perspective that the rest of us lack."

No shit I would. Neil is discussing how he and a few others have set up revision groups over the holiday. Quickly realise he's trying to elicit my help in finance and accounting, not fucking likely.

"No can do old boy, spending Christmas with the family, you know how it is. My brother's over from Australia so my mother's doing the whole family thing...no I'm actually off skiing next week. Sorry mate, next time."

Of course, there's only one set of exams so there won't be a next time. As for my brother Michael coming over, that's true, but I've fuck all intention of spending Christmas with him and his squealing brat. Ironically my parents' would probably roll out the red carpet for me this year. The same value system, built up over a lifetime's shared experiences as teachers, which made them view the

City with baffled distrust has prompted an outpouring of parental pride over my attendance here. The fact that the stuff we study bears no resemblance to anything they'd consider remotely useful is irrelevant. Almost worth it to turn up and gloat just to wind up Michael, not to mention ogle his Aussie wife, who is a bit tasty it has to be said, blonde hair and long tanned limbs. Far too good for him. The prospect of the assault on my senses from the toxic smells their two-year-old son releases remorselessly in my company seals it though. Once again I think I'll be paying a visit to Thailand's distant shores this Christmas.

"I was wondering if you'd look over my resume for me Harry? Maybe before the end of term so I could work on it over the holidays?"

Neil's looking at me anxiously, like I can actually be of some help to him. Truth is I can't. Know little about him but the slight edge of desperation in his voice tells its own story. He's given up a solid but dull job, I'm guessing a management accounting position with a Thames Valley based pharmaceutical company, cajoled his sceptical wife into putting a family on hold and gone heavily into debt. He's run the financial numbers on his spreadsheet, shown them to his wife, explaining it's a calculated risk. A way out of the sixty grand a year middle-class poverty trap. Now the rejection letters are starting to arrive on the doormat, waiting at home for him with an increasingly anxious wife after a twelve hour slog here. So it's a bowl of lukewarm pasta and a glass of cheap red wine before hitting the books for another couple of hours. By the bags under his eyes he's sleeping badly. Now Christmas is coming up, as well as the pressure of family and friends all asking what he's going to do when he finishes. But there's still hope and it comes in the form of the elusive City job offer. That's what he tells people, casually dropping names like Merrill Lynch and Lehman Brothers. Insinuating he's "in dialogue" with them.

"Got positive feedback from some hedge funds Harry. They recommended I look at starting the CFA in January."

"You know it takes three years, the failure rate's at least fifty percent."

"I know that, but together with taking finance electives on the MBA it should give me the edge."

"What age are you Neil, thirty-four?"

"Thirty-one. I've aged in the past few months..."

He laughs at this, pulling nervously at the remains of a bread roll.

"Why not go back to what you did before? Surely coming here'll help you with that? Go into the City and you'll be competing with kids ten years younger. Fuck that."

He shrugs and there are crumbs from the hard breadroll crust all over the white tablecloth.

"Maybe but, well… coming here is all about opening doors isn't it? Giving us choices?"

Won't tell you this because I know you'd hate to hear it, but the City deal's in human stock. If yours wasn't high enough to get your foot in the door in your twenties, they ain't gonna open it for you in your thirties. MBA or no MBA. Why do you think these investment banks and consultancies still ask for your A-level results? Social engineering mate that's why. Give Ethel her dues, she nailed it down straight when she tackled that consultancy chick earlier in term. Course they'll never admit to it. I fob him off instead with some meaningless fluff about the importance of bypassing HR and getting to speak to the decision maker. Load of shite actually but he's nodding his head sagely so he's obviously swallowed it. People usually do. The only reason HR departments exist is to protect the people on the front line from twats ringing them up wasting their time. Decide it'll be a laugh to give Neil my old Chief Investment Officer's name and tell him to make sure and mention mine. Best to call him in the afternoon mate. Old Gibbo's gonna fucking love that, back from a good lunch to a phone call from a revved up Neil asking for the opportunity to come in and discuss how his skill-set could be best utilised within KCT. Tempted to tell Neil just to turn up at the KCT office and not leave until he gets to present his credentials to Gibbo. Could prove dangerous though, the old bastard keeps two Purdy shotguns in his car and has threatened to use them more than once. Usually on some poor graduate trainee who's fucked up for the first and almost certainly last time. That's one of the problems with these MBA courses, they can't really prepare you to deal with the Gibbos of this world. Believe me, there's plenty of them out there.

Enough career advice for now. Develop a sudden fascination with the menu, although there's only so long I can feign interest in Cream of Mushroom Soup, Salmon in Lemon and Dill Sauce and Fresh Fruit Trifle. Pay best part of thirty grand for a few lectures, you think they'd throw in a decent meal now and again. No concept of customer service these academics. Course that'll all change when they're looking for our donations once we graduate and re-enter the world of gainful employment. They won't be able to do enough for us then. Well, they can rest assured they'll be getting fuck all out of me. Straightforward transaction as far as I'm concerned. Pay

65

my ridiculously inflated fees, enjoy my year, then notch it up on the CV. If I make a few contacts, business or social, for afterwards then well and good. Having managed to untangle myself from the torpor that constitutes conversation with Neil, I manage to catch an equally bored Stelio's eye and at last can have a proper grown-up conversation.

"Harry, my friend, you were lucky to qualify in the first place. Beckham's free kick against us in injury time at Old Trafford was a fluke, did he repeat it in Japan?"

"No, but he wasn't fully fit. Neither was Owen. Tell you what though, come this June, Euro 2004, we're gonna be awesome. You guys even qualified?"

"Of course we have. I tell you, Harry, Greece could surprise a few people. We have a good team spirit..."

Stelio's words drop off and his mouth drops open and I'm pretty sure it isn't in anticipation of the bread rolls they're passing around. Look behind me at what's caught his attention. It's Simone, making her way over here. Now that is a woman who knows how to dress for a party. Well spotted, Stelios mate. Now just play it cool Harry boy. This may well be the night you earn a very tasty dividend on that lump sum investment.

"Harry, sweetheart, how the fuck are you? You look great. It's just like really cool to see you. I'm just gonna sit down beside you for a moment, shoot the breeze with my old friend Harry."

What the fuck is she on? Actually I can guess. This could be interesting.

"This seating plan is just for shit, I mean they've put me next to some really tedious people. You and me Harry, we're not tedious people. Fuck it, I'm just gonna swap places with this chick, how do you pronounce this fucking name anyway?"

"It's Nakata, think she's Japanese, she's not here yet, but it's a great idea. I'm sure she won't mind and I certainly don't."

She smiles at me as she sits down turning to face me, this could definitely be game on.

"Absolutely, I mean they're like really polite people the Japanese, except when they bombed Pearl Harbour of course, but hey it's like Christmas we shouldn't talk about that. Let's talk about you Harry, you look great. You been working out? I bet you've been fucking lots of those young undergrads haven't you, you sly bastard?"

People are looking at us now, even Stelios looks a bit embarrassed. Maybe this wasn't such a great idea, I mean what the fuck do I say to that? Simone's clearly off her tits and I doubt she's going to come back down anytime soon. In fact as she's swapping the place settings her phone rings and she virtually bolts out the door almost knocking the MBA director, who's engaged in earnest conversation with Decker Honeycutt and Brett Rusk, a couple of Republican type US students, off his feet on the way. Well things could be worse. I could be sitting next to Brett and Decker talking about the radical agenda of the New Right. Think I'll stick with Simone and see how this plays out.

Danny McMullen

Someone bangs a gong calling us into dinner so I go look at the seating plan. Hey that's cool, I'm sitting beside Simone, way to go. Good idea a seating plan, otherwise dudes like me end up perched on the end of tables like a peasant at a wedding.

"Hello Danny, find where you're seating OK?"

It's the course director, pretty friendly dude really, about my age too. Interviewed me for a place here, ended up rapping about music. He's an acid jazz fan himself, not my kinda bag but each to their own and all that.

"Yeah, no probs."

"Good, we've lain on a little musical entertainment this evening, a string quartet. Not exactly the genre you prefer, but I hope you enjoy it anyway."

He smiles and moves seamlessly on to talk to someone else. Always amazes me how some dudes are just so comfortable in their own skin. I wander over to my seat, champagne in hand, couple of people speak to me on the way in and I'm starting to just chill out and enjoy myself. Most other people are already at the table, not Simone though. In fact, when I look at the name on the place setting beside me, it's not hers, it's Nakata's. She's in my study group. Got to know her pretty well because I did two years Japanese as a minor when I was an undergrad back in Canada and this is the first chance I've really had to use it regularly since. Weird or what though, could've sworn Simone's name was on the seating plan. Look around to see if I can see her. She's over beside Harry. Actually Nakata's there too. Hear raised voices, looks like there's a bit of a bad vibe over there. Think I'll go over and tell Simone that she's got her seating mixed up. I'm beginning to enjoy this evening, don't want things getting screwed up now.

Hope this dinner doesn't drag too long, not hungry, want to go to London and party. Would I do Harry? Bit short, not really built enough, but right now…yeah, it's not outta the question. Let's see if something else comes along though. Glad I swapped seats, keeps my options open. Where's the fucking dealer? What's the matter with this country, even the drug dealers don't want to make money?

"Excuse me, I think you sit in my seat. Go look at seating plan please, you in wrong seat."

What the fuck does this bitch want? This Japanese chick, must be that Nakata, arrives at my table and starts bitching and moaning that I'm sitting in her seat. Like I fucking care, tell her so as well. Now she's pissed at me, calling me "very rude lady", if she's not careful the slanty-eyed bitch'll get her ass kicked in a minute. Who does she think she is coming over to my table and creating a scene? Why should she care where she sits anyway? Now this other guy beside her, looks like a Jap as well, he's joining in. They're babbling away in Japanese, these people just have no manners.

Then that dumb-ass Canadian stoner Danny comes across, starts to act like some kinda UN secretary or something. He offers to swap seats with the Jap guy so he can sit with this Nakata bitch. Whatever, like I care, means I'm stuck with loser Danny, but big deal, long as he doesn't expect me to talk to him. This Nakata cow is clearly fucking this other Nip, so ask them why don't they just clear off to the bathroom and get it over with so the rest of us can have our dinner in peace. This pisses her off big time.

"You cheeky bitch, no-one like you, embarrassment to school, fuck off back to US."

OK then bitch bring it on! Danny starts talking to her and her skinny fuck-buddy in Japanese. That's typical of that waster, learn some dumb-ass language no-one else speaks. Lot of people are staring at us now, so embarrassing. Some people just have no idea how to behave, would never have happened at Stanford I can assure you. People knew how to conduct themselves in public there, fucking A they did. Shit, I hope that fucking dealer gets here soon. I'm on a come-down and there's no way I can sit through this charade straight. Phone goes again, finally he's here, about time too, fed me some bullshit line ten minutes ago that he was just around the corner, run outside.

"You're looking well fit tonight Princess, who's the lucky fella then?"

God this scumbags leering at me, gold tooth gleaming in his mouth. What does he look like in that check baseball cap, he's even got a fucking dog with him. One of those squat mean looking things. Looks like a sawn-off Pit Bull. Both of them are virtually foaming at the mouth, him over me, the dog 'cause I guess that's just what those things do. Still Billy's got what I need, gotta keep him sweet for now.

"I'm kinda busy Billy. I mean thanks for bringing the coke over but I need to get back in there, so just give me the stuff and here's the money."

"Hang on a sec, I come all the way over here, leave my mates in the boozer, and you ain't even gonna invite me and Lenny here in for a little drink. Not very sociable of you babe is it? Thought you and me were mates now, our little secret an' all that, eh?"

What the fuck's his problem? Why doesn't he just take the goddamn money and crawl back to whatever low-life cesspit he came from and take that deformed creature with him.

"Billy, be a sweetheart, don't mess me around here. I'd love to hang out with you, but you know what those assholes in there are like. They'll notice if I'm gone too long. Maybe come out here looking for me. Here, take the money."

"OK then, gorgeous. What nothing extra for a little Christmas drink? Tell you what, how about a little Christmas kiss instead for your mate Billy and we'll be sorted."

He lunges at me and the goddamn dog jumps up and starts nuzzling my thigh as well. Just as I get a waft of his beer-breath and push his grabbing hand off my ass someone comes outside. It's one of the business school secretaries. She smiles at me nervously as she lights a cigarette. Thank my lucky stars it's no smoking inside. Remember I had a run in with her once when she refused to do my photocopying. Like that's not her job? Thankfully I've already got the coke in my hand and this scumbag's taken the money. This transaction is concluded and dog and master skulk off into the night.

Danny McMullen

So anyway here we are seated at dinner. Like the course director says they've got a string quartet playing, quite chilled, find I'm enjoying myself. Everyone seems pretty relaxed after that little scene got defused. Y'know most people here are OK when you get to actually talk to them.

"So man you're from Lebanon? Never been there but it sounds like a pretty far out place from what I've heard before on the news and stuff. Kinda like Northern Ireland isn't it?"

...but he's telling me it's actually pretty cool now, real party vibe now, lots of clubs and stuff. Says there's even a good alternative music scene.

"Yeah, maybe I should come over and check it out. Lebanon; hey, that'd be well cool man, something to tell my daughter Caitlin about. Maybe even take a few records over and DJ a bit."

I could introduce the Lebanese to 'gaze, been ages since I DJ'd. Man I used to love it. Karen did too; it's how we first met. Back when I was at UCL, ten years ago now, I used to play once a month on a Wednesday night in a pub in Turnpike Lane. Little low-ceiling'd place where your feet stuck to the carpet. Doubt if more than fifty people ever came along, mostly students, but it was cool. Y'know, real chilled crowd. Used to spend all month putting my set together. Made sure it was a bit different every time. Course there were the classics that demanded to be played, 'black metallic', 'you made me realise', 'drive blind'. The sort of stuff you just don't fuck around with. But could still slip in something a little left-field. Bit of Sonic Youth or Floor. Was just rapping with some people at the bar after my set like I always did. Someone wanted to know what the final track I'd played was. Told them it was 'die, die, die' by Chapterhouse, a set-closer if ever there was one. Then Karen walked past. First thing I noticed was that she'd a little diamond stud in her nose, bit less common back then. Asked her if it hurt?

"Only the first time."

Then she smiled. Looked me straight in the eye as well, like she was deciding something important. Actually asked if she could buy me a drink and that was that. We were still talking at the bar an hour later when the lights came on and they called time. Moved in together after a couple of months and I decided to stay on in England. Means I never finished my PhD but no big deal. We were pretty happy. Never talked much about our relationship but we always seemed real comfortable together. Looking back we probably just gave each other an excuse to be lazy. I'd even given up the DJing before Caitlin came along a couple of years later. Money was a bit tight with Karen having to give up work and all that so I sold my decks. Never did get round to replacing them. Still got my turntable though, keeps me going for now. Hoping maybe this course'll get me up the ladder a bit at work. Might have a bit of spare cash for some new equipment. Decent mixer, another turntable, maybe one of those new professional CD players. Kind of forgotten about how much it all used to mean to me until I came to fill in my application form for this place. When they ask the "how you want to be remembered?" question. Said I'd like to be remembered DJing. Creating something by turning the back room of a rundown pub into a place where people wanted to come and hang out with each other, share their love of music, sometimes even get together and form their own bands. Try a little DJing, that kinda thing. Thought it was a good answer. Guess the dudes here musta like it too.

Like I said, everyone here at the table seems pretty chilled, except Simone. She's making me uncomfortable just sitting beside her, constantly jerking in her seat and pushing her food round her plate. She keeps disappearing and when she does talk to me she keeps stopping mid-conversation to butt into someone else's or just change the topic altogether. Course the topic usually revolves around her. This guy opposite me is from Kyrgyzstan. I'd vaguely heard of the place - knew it was a former Soviet Republic, but not much more than that. So this dude's telling us about it, how there're both US and Russian military bases there. Even tells us the US Peace Corps were in there, some real hot chicks from California and shit, bet that was a little bit of happiness for those Kyrgyz guys. Apparently, it's like a heavy strategic location because of where it's situated, real close to both China and Afghanistan. Got a load of gold, too. The whole region sounds like a bit of a powder keg with Islamic fundamentalism on the increase and so on, interesting stuff. But not to Simone, she keeps interrupting him to tell everyone how Stanford is like so superior to this place or how the UK is just like so antiquated compared to the States or how many job offers she's receiving. Wish she'd just cool it, it's boring. I keep telling myself there's something more beneath the surface and all that but now I'm not so sure. I guess I just like her 'cause she's hot.

Balbeck Toyevski

"So Balbeck, those Kyrgyz girls must have loved our Marines. I mean those guys are just hot. You know, I dated a guy for a while at Stanford and he ended up as an officer in the corps. I mean was he built or what. You got a girlfriend right? 'Course you do, cutie like you, but you better watch her 'round those guys. I tell you, man what I wouldn't do for a platoon of them here right now."

Did I not tell you this would be your opportunity to meet people? Now even Simone is paying attention to you. How foolish

71

you were to think she did not like you just because she did not acknowledge you often in the study group. She was just being professional, making sure things got done. You could learn from her. Soon you will be in a position of responsibility yourself back home. It is true what the business school say, you learn as much from the example of your classmates as you do in the classroom. That was why it was so important you studied abroad with clever people like Simone. Now it is obvious to everyone at the table that you are friends. Don't worry that you do not understand everything she says as she speaks very fast tonight and her accent is a little different than usual. That is just because she is excited to be here. Look at how her eyes sparkle and how she cannot stop talking to everyone. She's even grabbed your hand several times when she's talking to you. You do hope she is not feeling ill though because she has to leave the table quite often and has not eaten a lot of food. It is a shame for her because the food is very good tonight. It is so kind of the business school to provide the students with a dinner as a reward for all your hard work during the first term. The wine is very good too, it is not often you drink wine at home, but this is very nice. It is not so strong like vodka and it is easy to drink a lot of it. You must make a point of thanking the Dean personally for the hospitality you have enjoyed here tonight.

Listen carefully, Simone and the English guy beside her, Harry I think his name is, are talking about going to a party after the dinner. You should ask to come along as well. After all you are having such a lot of fun tonight and it is much too early to go home. Before you ask them though you decide to stand up and make a traditional Krygyz toast to your classmates. You smile when you think of the tales you will have to tell people back home about a night such as this.

Chapter Eight

Harry Stanton

OK it's almost 10pm and we need to get this show on the road quickly. Bloody dinner went on for longer than I thought but Jesus these speeches, they just go on and on. What a load of self-congratulatory crap. We know you're pleased to be here and we already know we all have a great future in front of us, we don't need you, Pablo from Peru, wasting 15 minutes of our fucking evening telling us all this, repeatedly. In fact so repeatedly that he's sweating profusely during his version of the Gettysburg address. Pablo finally sits down with streams of sweat trickling down his face and people thumping him on the back in encouragement. Now this little guy on our table is getting up. Bloody Hell, he's speaking in Russian or something. Not content with that, he's now translating his oration into English. He finishes off by lifting a full pint glass of lager someone's just reached him and downing it in one before pumping both fists in the air to a raucous ovation.

Now the Dean's on her feet smiling benevolently but the look on her face demands attention and the mood in the room changes perceptibly. Even Simone shuts up when the Dean starts talking.

"On behalf of myself and all the staff, thank-you for the invitation to join you this evening to celebrate the end of an outstanding term. Your presence here is physical evidence that our business school community is going from strength to strength. As participants on this programme you have a unique opportunity to learn from each other and truly develop global intellectual capital from a student body whose international diversity is second to none..."

Unfortunately, her flow is accompanied by the sound of Pablo demonstrating his intellectual capital by being violently ill. Testament to the Dean's professionalism she carries on regardless, only the briefest of grimaces acknowledging this untimely interruption .

"We, the faculty of the business school, seek to convert constraints into opportunities, to inspire leadership that involves the perfect combination of heart and mind, to push you over the cliff so you can fly..."

Some people are nodding their heads at the profound wisdom being imparted by the Dean. Others are trying to ignore the stench

73

of Pablo's alcohol induced vomit. The unfortunate Pablo, who now looks like he needs an appointment with a stomach pump, is being led unsteadily outside from where the sound of raised voices and further violent retching can be heard. Against these insurmountable odds, the Dean winds up her speech, wasting no time in making her excuses and leaving. She manoeuvres her way skilfully through both an increasingly drunken student body and Pablo's pool of vomit, her expressions of acknowledgement rather than encouragement enough to dissuade anyone seeking to make further demands on her time.

Right, that's it, had enough of this shite. Time to slip away from the table and put a call into the limo guy. Tell him to be outside in ten minutes. Need to round up the troops and make my own way out of here, problem is I can't see many of the original gang. At least Simone's up for it, quite possibly in more ways than one judging by the way we've been flirting all evening. There's Marianna over there, poured into that little black dress. Thankfully, generous donations of my time and expertise in the pursuit of helping her get her head around finance and accounting have meant I'm forgiven for that unfortunate misunderstanding in Wetherspoons earlier in term. She smiles and waves me over, excuse myself from the table again, a task made easier by Simone having vacated her place for one of her regular bathroom breaks.

"Hey Marianna, you look amazing babe, I love that dress. Listen a few of us are going dancing in London. I know you like to dance, come with us, there's a car picking us up outside in a few minutes."

"Harry I can't, I'm sorry, I need to get up early in the morning to study, you know how worried I am about the exams."

What's this garbage she's spouting, don't these people understand what this year is really all about?

"Come on Marianna, you've worked so hard all term you deserve to party, little cheeky tequila, some dancing. Come on, I'll look after you, you've got the whole holiday to study...oh come on please, just for me? Ok, listen, remember what I told you about the capital asset pricing model? Maybe now's the time to take on some extra risk."

She looks at me with a smile that's just maybe tinged with regret.

"Harry, you're so sweet but you already know the answer."

It's a classy put-down, laced as it is with just a hint of arrogance. Even more so when she informs me her fucking boyfriend's arriving next week so she has to study now so she can spend 'quality time' with him. Well fuck that for a game of soldiers, I spend half the term helping the dozy bitch grasp the basic fundamentals of double entry bookkeeping, then some gringo flies halfway round the world and gets to enter her. There's no justice in this world. Adios then senorita, shame, it has to be said she is a sweet kid.

Simone's back at the table, time to get a grip on this situation. If the others have fucked off somewhere else then that's their lookout. What am I, a fucking taxi service? Anyway, make it easier if it's just me and Simone. Game on!

Danny McMullen

I'm feeling a bit drunk now man, what I really fancy is a spliff but I didn't bring any. Guess I could go back home and get some but that's a drag. I'm having a good time here, don't really want to bail out yet. Maybe I'll call Miguel, he's not here as it's MBAs only tonight, no civilians allowed. Lives close by though and he'll sort me out. Always has plenty around. Better go outside to call him though. Wasn't gonna bring my mobile, glad I did now.

Shit, he's not in. Trying to think of who else could help out. Maybe I'll just head home. That's a bummer though, tonight's the first time I've actually felt like I belong here. Still I do fancy a toke.

"Alright mate, you off on this shindig to London then? Car's here all ready when you are."

Look around but there's no-one else there so guess they must be talking to me. Two dudes in a big white limo. Think I recognise one of them, the one who was talking to me. Sure he works in the canteen at business school. About to say no, they're looking for someone else, when I get a whiff of a real sweet smell coming from the car. Pretty familiar too. Unless I'm very much mistaken, these two dudes have got some prime Skunk on the go. Usually a bit of a head-fuck for my tastes, but tonight I could be persuaded. Approach the car and lean in the open window.

"Hey there, just wondering whether you guys got any of what you're smoking going spare? Man I'm just craving a toke. Any chance I can have a drag, maybe buy a little off you?"

The driver, big guy, dressed in a dark suit and white shirt with no neck-tie, says sure, have a draw, plenty more where that came from. I do, fuck it's strong. He asks where I'm from and we start rapping. Decide to buy an eighth, not cheap this stuff, but it's good gear. Like I said earlier, I feel like getting ripped tonight. Worried in case someone comes out and catches me toking so jump in the back of the car. Next thing, Harry, Simone and Balbeck climb in.

Simone's clinging to Harry's arm as she topples onto the back seat, her already short dress rising up somewhere round her waist. Harry's looking very pleased with himself, while Balbeck's a bit glassy eyed and his face reddens when I catch him staring at Simone's endless legs.

"Allright mate, your lot all here then?"

There's a hint of a challenge in the driver's voice.

"That's us, we're all set, need to get cracking though it's almost 10:30."

He just grunts at this, checking out Simone's arm linked in Harry's before lowering his gaze to her legs. The skinny dude alongside him who I recognise from the canteen's also turned to face us. They smirk at each other before Harry pulls the partition screen shut.

"Hang round here any longer and the evening's gonna be wasted. Don't want that do we babes?"

Harry's now got his arm round Simone's waist as he says this. Must have cost him to lay on this little trip. This is a big old limo, got leather seats, TV, well stocked mini-bar, CD player. The car starts up and some booming R'n'B music comes pounding out of the speakers behind us. Not usually a great fan of this but must say it goes well with the hash and the booze.

"Allright ladies and gentlemen, let's get this party started, raise your glasses please."

Harry's produced a bottle of champagne from the mini-bar and four glasses, this is all for Simone's benefit though, he barely acknowledges Balbeck and I. Still, not about to turn down some free champagne am I?

"Anything else you guys need back there to help the party along?"

The skinny dude's opened the partition window and is grinning at us. It's obvious it's not beer and peanuts he's offering. There's a dog in the front as well, its stuck its broad head through the partition and I swear it's grinning at us. I go to pet him though and the fucker growls at me.

"Man, is that your dog? He's one of those Bull Terriers isn't he? I love dogs, we always had them as kids when I was growing up back in Canada. They don't fuck you over like people. What's his name?"

"Lenny. Yeah, he's a Staffie. Fuckin' well 'ard too. Ripped a retriever's ear off the other day. Served it right, was off the lead weren't it? Came over to Lenny giving it the big one, got an ear tore off for its trouble. I says to the geezer, ain't my fault mate, my dog was on the lead, go and get the Old Bill if you want, won't do no

76

fucking good. Most of the time he's good as gold though, wouldn't hurt a fly would you, boy?"

"Hurt that fucking retriever though, didn't he mate?"

That's the big dude, obviously approves of Lenny's pugilistic streak. Looks like he probably shares it too. Lenny, though, looks pretty chilled at this point, thumping his tail on the floor as Simone wriggles half-way through the partition, and half-way out of her tight silver dress as well. Wouldn't have figured on Simone being a dog lover but her and Lenny seem like old pals.

"Got any Es then Billy? If we're going dancing, they'd go down real well. Get loved up and party."

She starts waving her arms in the air as she says this. I'm sure the guys upfront are enjoying this little show. The one driving, real cool dude, he's grinning at her, she's checking him out too. There's some real vibes here. Wonder how Harry boy's gonna like this little turn of events?

"Sure gorgeous, anything for you. Open up for me then."

Simone opens her mouth and Billy pops a pill in it. Man she's already high in the sky. Still, she recoils when he runs his finger over her lips. There's a joint doing the round and she's been toking on it too, we all have apart from Harry and Balbeck. Thing is, I used to really dig ecstasy back in my clubbing days. Karen and I used to do it at home as well, before Caitlin came along. Fuck it, it's time for some late night accoutrements.

"I'll take one of those as well man. How much, anyway?"

"Just call it a fiver, seeing it's Christmas and we're all mates."

Fuck, that's cheap. I remember paying fifteen quid for these things not so long ago. Might as well buy two. Just shows you how long I've been away from this kinda scene. Bet these things are common as candy now. Pay the man, pop the pill, and prepare to party.

Simone Sanders

God this dinner is interminable, end, end, end, so I can go and party. Where's that damn waiter anyway? Need more liquor to drown out the drone of this guy beside me's voice in my ear.

"America's facing an epidemic of anxiety. Over education, social status, physical attractiveness, take your choice. Surely studying here must give you a better appreciation of the advantages of the European social model, Simone?"

Advantages of anything European? As if.

"That's a crock of shit. I mean the difference between here and the States is that people just take more personal responsibility over there, y'know. I mean take me. I'm successful because I'm smart, I work hard. I don't expect hand-outs from the Government. I mean that's what this whole MBAs about, right? Making you guys think like Americans."

There, that told him. Nothing like the sound of an American accent to get these losers all riled up.

'America needs to consider this, America needs to ask itself that.' Swear they're like a broken record these losers.

America's like, totally fine without your pissy advice. Amazing over here you even get Commies at business school. Like hello, what exactly did you think you were coming here to study? Gotta blame it on the faculty though, mean they set the tone. Dress like undergrad students and invite a whole load of do-gooders to come and preach to the class on the need for enlightened capitalism and what kinda message are you giving out? Not that I'm a Bush supporter or anything. That guy's just a jackass. Hard to believe he did an MBA, especially at Harvard, and that's where that asshole from Ledbetter Capital hires from? Must have shit for brains. Mind you gets me thinking, maybe I should set my sights a bit higher than some half-assed hedge fund that's probably gonna go under in twelve months. Yeah, Simone for president! When I get home I'm gonna ring that asshole back and tell him he's just dinged the future president of the USA. Let him shove that up his ass. Someone else gets up to make a toast, fuck that. I disappear to the bathroom for some refuelling. There's only so much earnest discussion a girl can take. Especially with a skinny, lank-haired loser you'd rather hammer nails through your hand than fuck. Get a spoonful up each nostril and I'm ready to go. Tonight I feel like dancing, yeah, haven't been out properly in a while, been too busy here, but not tonight.

"Hello Simone, are you enjoying yourself tonight? Certainly seems quite lively over on your table."

Fuck, it's the Dean! Shit how long's she been in here? Hope she didn't hear me snorting in the stall, shit, is there any of this powder on my fucking nose? That little Mexican bitch that dresses like a slut slinks past and out the door, throwing me a look on the way. What am I sweating it for, it's just the Dean. I mean, like, I pay her wages, right?

"Oh, we're just letting off a bit of steam, Dean. Everyone's been working so hard this term. I was up all night myself working on today's presentation, you guys just push us so hard here. I guess that's what happens when you sign up for a one year program. Still, it'll be good preparation for back in the real world. I mean, I thrive on pressure, unlike some of the others. You know, if you're really going to maximise the potential of this business school I think you need to look at your admission's policy. I mean, some people here have spent like their entire careers working for the government. "

There, that fucking told the snotty bitch. About time someone did, honest to God some of the deadheads they let in here are a disgrace. Not much wonder our business school rankings are for shit. Better watch I don't sue them if they keep slipping. Wanted a mid-table school I'd have stayed at home and gone to Tippie, saved a fortune too. Almost tell her that, but decide to wait, another opportunity will come.

"We aim for diversity Simone, cultural, social and professional diversity. We feel it's a key competitive advantage of the school. It's important the students who graduate from here accept that. We are not interested in the race to the top competition that characterises so much of higher education today, particularly in the US."

Well, fuck me! There's a tone in this bitch's voice I don't like, looks like she's stepping up to the plate. Decide not too push it. What is that old Chinese dude says? If your enemy is superior, split and come back another time or something? Remember it from *Wall Street*.

"Completely agree Dean, no one is more committed to the ideals of this school than me. Anyway, I better get back to the others. I think we're going on to party in London afterwards. Harry's organised it."

What am I telling her that for? Too much information, this stuff does that to you.

"Of course, just be careful Simone, you don't want to overdo the partying if you're exhausted from your work schedule. Might be an idea just to relax and take it easy for a while."

Fuck, is this bitch onto me? Why's she staring at me like that? Shit, I could get my ass slung out of here if she suspects. Turn away to wash my hands and then get the fuck out of the bathroom. Harry needs to get his fucking ass in gear and get us out of here quick.

Back at the table, it looks like we're finally on the move, hallelujah. Seems like Balbeck's coming as well. Whatever, just need to get away from these boring fucks, act like they're at the school prom or something. Get outside and the limo's waiting, very nice, Harry's got style I'll give him that. Pissed to see that loser Danny's tagging along again though, doesn't he have any friends? Wait a second, check out this driver. Well hello there, this dude is fucking built, tall, shaven headed, looks like one of those Russian secret service hard-bodies you see in the movies. Bet he can go all night. He's checking me out too. Looks me right in the eye and holds my stare, looks me up and down real slowly then just smiles and nods slightly, then gets out and holds the door open for me. My dress rides up when I sit down but so what, this guy is into me and no mistake.

So off we go. Pretty comfy in here and Harry's cracked open the champagne, might do another snort in a minute, not like any of this lot are gonna turn me in. Danny's smoking a joint of some real strong smelling stuff, try a little of that too, but doesn't really agree with me. I want to be up on a positive vibe not zoning out. In fact, the thought of going dancing and getting all hot and sweaty with this guy up front makes me think of having an E. Just then Billy, who for some reason is riding up front as well, together with his evil looking mutt, asks if we have any special requirements. Well whadda y'know, just so happens I have and Billy's able to meet them. Wash down the pill with some water that Billy produces, then decide it's time I got to know our driver a little better.

"So Billy, didn't know you were in the limo business?"

"It's my mate here's, I just come along to keep him company, don't I."

"So does your 'mate' here have a name?"

Billy and the driver exchange grins, he's looking at me in the rear view mirror as he speaks.

'I'm Rio, you must be Simone. Billy's told me all about you. Didn't tell me you were this gorgeous though."

Cheesy but effective. Looks like I may be in for a little bit of loving tonight, about time too.

"Did he not? Well maybe he doesn't think I'm all that pretty, is that it Billy, I'm not your type? What about you Rio? What's your type, or maybe you're not into girls. Is that it, you and Billy an item then?"

Billy doesn't like this, looks like he'd like to slap me. Rio though plays it much cooler, just smiles.

"I'm into women, not girls. Maybe I'll show you just how much I'm into them a bit later, let you find out for yourself."

He's looking at me in the rear view mirror as he says this, greedily and deliberately, swear to God I think I'm blushing.

"Will you now? So is that a threat or a promise? I've been let down before by guys talking the talk but not delivering."

We're stopped at traffic lights now and he's turned round to face me.

"Well you ain't gonna have to worry 'bout that on this occasion."

"Hey mate, shut that fucking partition and give us some privacy in here would you! Remember who's paying for this evening."

Oh dear, Harry is not a happy bunny. Can tell Rio's pissed at this but just smiles at me and closes the partition. Damn, still the evening's not over yet, we'll be in London real soon and this is getting interesting. Got a hunch the back of this limo's seen it's share of action. Mood I'm in, maybe it'll see a bit more real soon.

"Hey Harry, lighten up, we were just having a little fun that's all, don't be such a grinch."

He looks pissed though. Better watch it, don't want this evening to end abruptly, not now it's going so well. Men are just so fucking childish sometimes.

Harry Stanton

So what's the fucking deal here then? I shell out a couple of hundred quid to these clowns and then this prick tries to shag the one bit of female company I've managed to bring along. Tomorrow morning I'm straight on the phone to this lot making sure this asshole's out on his ear if they want any more business from me. Thing is, Simone seems well into Mr Loverman in front, must have a thing for shaven headed gorillas or something. Anyway, I'm paying for this little shindig, so I'm calling the shots, end of.

"Right guys, here's the plan. We'll start off at my club, Lonsdale in Notting Hill first, have a couple of drinks there then maybe head over to Chinawhite. I'm a member there as well, so I'll try and get you all in, depends how busy they are. If not, then it'll just be me and Simone. Sure you two can amuse yourselves for a couple of hours in London."

Too fucking right they can. No way I'm signing dopehead and the man from Kyrgyzstan into Chinawhite. No intention of going there myself. Plan is to have a few drinks with Simone alone upstairs in Lonsdale then take her back to my flat in Notting Hill. I've rented one of the rooms out to Mark who I used to work with as he's going through a divorce. His missus caught him in a compromising situation with one of our temps, young Charmaine from Hackney, very tasty too. Was taking the wife out to Sketch for their anniversary, so Mark books a suite at the Great Eastern as she wants them to stay up in town afterwards. Being a value investor he decides he may as well get full use of it given all the coin he's shelled out, so takes Charmaine over there for a mid-afternoon treat. Unfortunately for Mark, wifey arrives up in town early intending to surprise him. She turns up with her new purchase from Agent

Provocateur, walks in the suite and catches him in the Jacuzzi mid-stroke with Charmaine, who needless to say isn't wearing a swim-suit. Oh dear. One very expensive divorce pending and he's crashing at my gaff. Well, helps pay the mortgage and added bonus that he's still screwing Charmaine, so I get copious opportunities to check out her navel pierced mid-riff. Of course, I've still got my flat for weekends when I come down here, complete with King size bed, which I intend to put to very good use tonight.

"What about Rio and Billy, they gonna come too?"

What the fuck does Danny care whether they come, didn't have him down for a poof.

"No can do I'm afraid, can only sign a couple of members in at a time, very exclusive these places I'm taking you too. That OK with you babe?"

Simone nods, she's swigging the water now, then raps the partition to ask Billy for some gum. Still the old ecstasy should get her in the mood for it and no mistake. Lonsdale is well cool, needs to be for the coin they charge, get her upstairs in there and she'll soon forget all about that lowlife up front. We're driving through North East London now, fucking grim and no mistake. All these foreigners on our course want to see the real Britain, take a look out the window. No Starbucks, Pret a Manger or Pizza Express here, just abandoned cars, graffiti, concrete tower blocks, cheap take-aways, taxi firms, everything for a pound shops. Who the fuck lives like this? Remember back when I stared in the City as a graduate trainee, seems like a lifetime ago now, really fancied one of the receptionists. Lisa her name was, dead fit and flirty with it, used to play up to the young guys no end. Wasn't a Monday morning you didn't get an account of her sexual Olympics over the weekend. Nothing too graphic, just enough detail to make sure there was a steady stream of male visitors to the reception desk. Plenty of them top brass too. Got away with murder in her timekeeping did Lisa, well looked after at bonus time too. Anyway, one time she invites me to a house party, Edmonton way, around here somewhere. I'd been to Uni in Leeds so I wasn't completely naïve, not like some of the other chumps we'd employed. Still a bit of an eye-opener though, old ecstasy scene was in full swing then, people pilled up to the eyeballs. Some heavier shit than that going around too. Hung around for a while trying and failing to fit in, desperate not to look like a prick, then I finally saw Lisa. Unfortunately she was disappearing into the bedroom giggling with some meathead with his hand up her virtually non-existent skirt. Fucked off home after that, following Monday Lisa asks me if I'd been there, says some of her friends reckoned I might have been. Told her I was but she looked busy. She just raised her eyebrows and I knew then it'd been a lost cause from the start. Stayed mates for a while though 'til she changed jobs, back then I was a bit more broad minded. Actually bit more naïve's probably more accurate. Mood in the car's a bit quieter now, even Simone seems to have momentarily calmed down. Balbeck's hardly said a word since he got in, think this might be a bit more than the poor lad can handle. Probably end up staying in the car with Pinky and Perky up front. Need to liven things up a bit.

"Right, we're almost there, the fun's about to begin lady and gentlemen. Let's have a little sharpener shall we?"

Open another bottle of champagne, fill their glasses up and ten minutes later we're pulling up outside Lonsdale. Simone's got her lipstick out now and is applying a generous coating of its blood red colour to her lips, then starts combing her hair pretty vigorously. Looks like she's revving up again, no doubt that E's starting to kick in. Tell the others I'll sort out entrance. Once inside, explain to the fashionista controlling entrance that I want to take one guest to the private upstairs lounge and I've got a few other mates with me who'll just drink in the downstairs bar. They're cool with that. Fucking good job as well the amount I've spent in here the past couple of years.

"OK guys, can only sign one guest upstairs, but persuaded them to allow you two to have a drink downstairs. You'll enjoy it, some amazing eye candy in there. Could be your lucky night Balbeck, have high hopes for you."

Now Simone's asking me about the two up front. She's having a laugh, sure I'll sign them into Lonsdale, they can bring the fucking dog as well.

"Unfortunately they won't be able to join us on this occasion, it's a very selective door policy. Anyway, they need to stay with the car, can be quite a dodgy neighbourhood round here."

We get out of the car and go into the bar. Slightly tricky moment as the fashion fascist on the door scrutinises Balbeck's shoes, which come resplendent with tassles. Thankfully, together with a dinner suit that's a good two sizes too big, he's just about retro enough to be trendy in this part of London and gets waved through. I guide Simone towards the upstairs lounge, while pointing the other two firmly in the direction of the much less exclusive ground floor bar. Once upstairs, nod to a couple of faces I know from my City days. Catch them oogling Simone, even though they've got some eye candy of their own. Usual type, all straight-ironed hair and skinny arms. Simone and I settle into a private booth and I order us a bottle of Dom Perignon. Her eyes are like saucers now, her make-up's starting to run a bit as well and her face is covered in a thin film of sweat. Just makes me want her all the more to be honest. The skinny blonde waitress looks at her knowingly when she takes our order. Mind you they see all kinds of casualties in here.

"You know Simone, I've always had the feeling there's unfinished business between us after that afternoon when I helped you get rid of your ex's stuff. We've just never had a chance to be on our own. Now we do."

"Harry, I don't know. I mean, I'm not sure I wanna get involved with someone on the program…"

"Simone c'mon, we're not like the rest of these muppets on the course. You and I, we're different, we know the score. That's why we should be together. Right from the first time we met in the lift there's been something between us."

I'm looking right into her eyes when I say this. I move my left hand onto her thigh, she doesn't recoil, with my right hand I stroke her cheek, she swallows and looks down at her silver painted toe-nails. I find myself staring at her ankles. They're perfect. Even if they were all I saw of her, I'd want her. Have to rip my eyes away from them or I'll be lost for words.

"You know my London flat's just round the corner from here. How about we finish up this and go back there? It's a lot more private."

"OK…I guess so. Let me just pop to the bathroom first Harry, freshen up a bit. I'll be right back."

"Don't worry, I'm not going anywhere."

She's unsteady on her feet and initially totters off in the wrong direction towards the exit rather than the toilets. Panic momentarily, thinking she's changed her mind and is leaving, then she gets pointed in the right direction by our waitress. The couple at the next table are looking at her. The bloke feigning to share his fat girlfriend's disapproval when he's really leering at Simone's vastly superior arse. Lean back in the padded leather booth, take the champagne out of the ice bucket and top up Simone's lipstick smeared flute. Take a sip of my own and savour the moment. The blonde waitress struts past, all legs and lips. I smile at her but she gives me a contemptuous glare in return. What's that in aid of? Who gives a fuck, anyway. It's all up for grabs with Simone now. I've taken it easy on the booze as always, just a question of getting her back to mine. We'll grab a cab. Don't want that randy bastard of a driver fucking up my well laid plans.

Whoah! This is like too much, way too much. Need to get to the bathroom now. Not sure if I can make it, my heart's pounding so hard it's nearly knocking me off my feet. Just need to take a time out here. I'm fucking throbbing though. Get into a cubicle and get my hands between my legs. This damn thong's soaked through. Goddam Harry. I'm on heat here. If I let that bastard fuck me he better do it properly after all this. Like Travis used to back in Tipton. Shit I used to wet myself just watching him lift weights. He musta bench-pressed 180 effortlessly. The way he used to just take the bar to a millimetre off his chest then take it up slowly and evenly. Then it would be my turn. He took 5lbs off me, gave me a line down the middle of my gut that looked like he'd taken a chisel to. People used to ask me if I was living in the gym. Truth is, I damn near was. Just so I could get up close to him. Those abs, that ass. That cock, that glorious all-American cock. Hoisting me up so my legs were wrapped round his broad back. Biting my nipples. Then lowering me onto him. The sweat dripping off my face and pouring down my neck. Splatting onto the wooden bench as he fucked me in the sauna. The pressure from his strong hands gripping me harder just before he'd come. Making me feel like just staying there in Tipton. With him putting his seed inside me. OHMIGOD. Shit that was good. Just sit back and take five here. Get my head together. Try and get my breathing under control. Get out of the cubicle and run some cold water in the sink.

"Excuse me, it's like none of my business and all that, but are you OK?"

It's the waitress who brought our drinks. Sounds American too.

"Sure I'm fine. Just a bit tired. Been a long day, y'know…"

"Right, sure. It's just…well you don't look OK. That guy you're with, you know him, right?"

"Harry? Yeah of course, he's a friend. We're at school together. Look I'm fine. I've just had a bit too much to drink. Y'know how it goes, right?"

"OK, if you're sure…"

She kinda hangs a second or two looking uncertain, then shrugs and leaves. Not like I asked her to start getting involved or anything. Looking in the mirror though I see why she did. Even in this subdued lighting my face tells its own story. So what? Apply a fresh coat of lipstick, tie my hair back in a pony tail and pop back into the cubicle for a little pick me up. Harry'll still be there when I get out.

Balbeck Toyevski

In the car you start to feel a little tired from all the alcohol that you have drunk and now they are smoking hashish. You have tried this a couple of times in Bishkek but do not like it. That stuff makes your head spin. Now you are thinking that maybe you should not have come on this trip. Simone seems very wild and you are concerned that things might get a little out of control. However, you are here now and should try to enjoy yourself. Do you want to ruin the evening for the others by being selfish?

The car pulls up outside a bar in London, you have not been to this area before. You are a little nervous of going inside in case you do not fit in and people stare at you, but after all you are all guests of Harry's and it would be rude to refuse his hospitality. So you should enter and have a drink. It is good for you to experience life outside of the University. This is one of the reasons you came to England. Harry and Simone go upstairs and you are left downstairs with Danny. The bar is very crowded and it is taking a long time for Danny to get served. While he is getting the drinks, you look around, it is quite dark inside and it must be difficult to talk with the loud music in the background. It is strange but the people are not dressed very smartly. Danny and you are the only people wearing ties. You also hear a couple of girls at the bar speaking Russian. They are very beautiful, one of them is wearing a white top that looks like a bra. She has long dark hair that falls down over her shoulders and she's sipping her drink through a straw while looking round the room. You know it is rude to stare but cannot help yourself. She catches you looking but does not smile, instead looking you up and down dismissively before saying something to the tall blonde haired girl beside her. The blonde haired girl looks over at you and they both laugh. You are embarassed and feel your face turning red. Danny is talking to another pretty girl at the bar, who is laughing at what he is saying. Finally the barman comes to you instead and asks what you want to drink. You decide to order four bottles of beer as the two guys driving the car have came in to the bar. They are talking to some people, it is only polite to buy them both a drink too.

Danny McMullen

Damn, I'm coming here more often. Gotta make a point of thanking Harry. Great guy really, sorting it out for us to get in here. Reckon we've become real good buddies now. Same with Simone. Just a question of getting to know people. Think I'll give them both some 'gaze CD's for Christmas. Balbeck too. Signing up for this MBA's turning out to be one of the best moves I've ever made. Hanging out with these guys, coming to places like this. It's awesome in here. Talk about hot women, the music's really slamming too. In that far corner there's a girl with straight blonde hair, she looks like PJ Harvey man, except PJ's got dark hair. Whatever dude, she's fucking beautiful, I wanna have her babies. For a second I feel a bit overdressed in this dinner suit, especially when everyone else's pulling off that distressed casual look which probably costs about a year's course fees to perfect. But so what, not like anyone really gives a shit, is it? Man this bar's crowded, gonna take a while to get served. That's fair enough though, don't expect the barmen to ignore the pouting female customers and come rushing over and serve me. No problem, I'm just pure enjoying being part of all this. Can't wait to tell Harry how much I appreciate this. Feel like just going and finding the guy and hugging him. This chick at the bar beside me's amazing looking. We're pushed up pretty tight against each other. She's smiling at me now. Turns out she's from Belgium, tells me she's bisexual. Every now and then she and her girlfriend pick some lucky guy up from a bar and take him back for a threesome. Reckon she's just rapping with me but that's cool, makes a change from being ignored.

"So, like, how do I apply for this position of being you ladies' sex toy?"

She laughs and tosses her hair. Redheads are gorgeous.

"You're sweet, where are you from?'

"Canada, but I've lived in London for years. Now I'm at Business School though."

"Yeah, Business School, smart guy too, I like that. I'm a web-site designer. What's you name?"

"Danny, so what do you design? Let me guess - you're real trendy, it's gotta be fashion sites right?"

"Nope"

"OK, music then, has to be music or maybe books, something creative?"

"Nope, keep guessing though."

"I'm thinking movies, yeah movies or maybe travel? You kinda look like you've travelled a lot."

She's smiling and nodding now, not sure if it's 'cause I've guessed right or 'cause she's decided to screw me. Either way, bulls-eye Danny Boy, think she likes me. Maybe she's not kidding. Never had a threesome before. I'll pop that other pill on the way over to their place, been sitting round feeling sorry for myself for far too long. That stops right now.

"Come here then Danny, and I'll tell you exactly what I do."

"Hey man, what the fuck?"

Someone grabs me from behind by the collar of my jacket just as I bend down to let her whisper in my ear. Then I'm pulled forcefully towards the door through a crowd of people who get out of the way pretty damned quick.

"You guys just think you can come in here and start dealing? This is a private members' club. You ever show your faces in here again and we're calling the police, got that?"

I get physically thrown out on the street where I find Balbeck and the two dudes driving the car already out there. Balbeck looks bewildered, the other two look like they're considering taking this further. Now they're engaged in a full scale Mexican stand-off with the doormen. Fuck man, this is not the action I was hoping for two minutes ago.

"Who the fuck do you think you are, treating your members like this? The owner's a personal friend of mine, tomorrow morning first thing you're gonna lose your fucking job, you muppet."

Harry's being slung out on his ass too. Simone, looking increasingly dishevelled, is joining in for good measure.

"I'll sue your ass you fuck, you twisted my arm going down those stairs. You are in a world of trouble you just don't know it yet."

"You, yeah you, what the fuck do you think you're doing dealing drugs in my club? Think they're gonna tolerate that from a loser like you? Just get in the fucking car and drive me and her to my flat. The rest of you can fuck off to wherever for all I care."

Harry's having a right go at this Rio dude, think he better cool it a bit, this guy's one mean looking hombre. He's just staring at Harry now, looks like he could pulp him without pausing for breath and no mistake. Shit man, better try and calm things down a bit.

"Hey guys, things are just getting a little out of hand. Why don't we just move on somewhere else and chill out a bit. C'mon everybody, just relax."

Rio prowls up to Harry, moving lightly on his feet. He's a good four inches taller and menacing with it.

"You've got a big mouth, cunt. You been giving me grief all the way down here. I've had enough of your shit, give me my money and find your own fucking way home or I'm gonna fucking hurt you."

Harry's not looking so confident now as Rio just stands in front of him blocking his way back into the club. Balbeck and even Simone look concerned. Billy's smirking in the background, he's got the dog out of the car as well. This is turning into a nightmare gig. Harry's looking toward the door of the club but the doormen don't want to know. Easy, Harry, just pay the dude, we'll all be alive to get the train home in the morning.

"OK mate take it easy. Look, I've already put it on my account but here ..."

He's going through his wallet nervously, drops it on the ground. Billy picks it up and gives it to Rio who takes a handful of notes out, looks like a fair sum.

"...take what's there, that should cover it, if not, take the others home and they'll give you the rest."

What's Harry playing at, dude there ain't no way I'm getting back in a car with these two.

"I don't give a fuck what you've paid on account, and I ain't taking any of these wankers home, except for her if she still wants to flash her tits at me. Like I said, give me my money, you booked my limo you're gonna pay for it. Me and Billy here we're expecting a tip for all our inconvenience. I'm trying to be patient but keep pushing it and you're gonna get a slap."

Simone's gone white now, in fact she staggers off behind the car somewhere and starts throwing up.

"OK mate, whatever you say. Look, I gotta go to the cash-point on the Portobello Road though and get the rest. It's only round the corner, OK?"

Rio nods at Harry, then opens the door, glowering at us as we get in before slamming it shut behind us. We hear the dull thud of the central locking being switched on as Rio drives off. Billy turns around grinning at us and offers Simone a stick of the gum he's chewing but she just snivels and shakes her head. There's a morbid silence in the car and my innards are churning. The smell of the hashish is still in the air but it's sickly now. Two empty champagne bottles lie on the floor in the back. This party ended a while ago. We pass a couple of police cars, but what the fuck would we say? It's not like we're getting mugged, is it? My heart's beating so loud it's like Loz Colbert's back beating the skins for Ride. Simone's silently retching, cocaine and fear combining. Strangely, only

Balbeck seems calm, just looking straight ahead of him like he's accepted something bad's going down.

We stop at the HSBC and Harry gets out. The two dudes and Lenny, who somehow has morphed in the past few minutes from man's best friend into an evil looking fucker, get out with him. Simone starts sobbing, then grabs hold of me.

"Shit Danny, what the fuck are we gonna do? You've seen the way that guy's been looking at me. What if that animal tries to rape me?"

Cocaine paranoia kicking in here and no mistake. As for me, any pleasant narcotic experience I was having disappeared along with the doorman's escort out of the bar.

"Just stay calm. He won't, Balbeck and I are here. Harry's pissed him off and he just wants his money that's all. Once he's been paid he'll let us go and we can all go back to Harry's and wait for a train in the morning."

She's looking at me all wild-eyed now. Don't blame her, last time I saw physical action was on a Canadian college rugby field. Getting creamed by a 220lb Saskatoon farmboy's gonna be a walk in the park compared to tackling this Rio guy. Still, need to do something, anything, to keep her from losing it big time.

"The doors are unlocked so let's all get out of the car together. Be ready to leave once Harry's paid him. We'll look for a cab. Just stick together, we'll be OK?"

I look over at Balbeck but he's not in the car. I climb out and grab Simone's arm pulling her out after me. On the street, Harry's handing over some money to this Rio dude, who has him backed up against a wall, looks like a serious amount too. This has been an expensive evening for him, all things told. Then Rio says something I can't quite catch, grabs Harry by his jacket lapels and head-butts him. Harry staggers back and slumps down the wall, blood pouring through his hands which are covering his face and turning his white dress shirt crimson. I step forward and tell Billy to just take the money and go, they've had their fun. He sneers but then the sneer becomes frozen on his face as Rio lurches backwards onto the main road holding his throat, like he's been punched in the windpipe. Balbeck is moving towards him on the balls of his shoeless feet, suddenly he leaps in the air and lands a perfectly placed kick on Rio's chest, knocking him straight into the path of an oncoming police van. The van skids in the rain but Rio takes its impact full on, crumpling him like a cardboard carton. The van's headlights illuminate his motionless body through a curtain of rain. I'm no doctor but I'll bet my entire 'gaze collection this dude's dead on impact.

90

Chapter Nine

Simone Sanders

"Listen officer, I've already told you what happened. It was an accident. These guys had an argument with Harry then attacked him. We were just defending ourselves. To be honest, none of it had anything to do with me. I was just an innocent bystander. Look, I'm kinda beat here, when you guys gonna let me go?"

"But you'd been in their car, travelling with them and now one of them is dead because your friend attacked him and kicked him into the street. Surely you can understand why we need to pursue this line of inquiry, Miss Sanders?"

"Sure, but Balbeck's not my friend; I hardly know the guy. As for those two low-lifes, they were trying to get money from Harry. They said he owed them for driving us to London. They got nasty, threatened me, then attacked Harry."

"There were a lot of illegal drugs in their car: cocaine, ecstasy, cannabis. Do you know anything about how they came to be there?"

"Hell no, I don't do drugs. You've already searched me."

The cop asking the questions looks first at me, then at this duty solicitor they've given me, then at his female colleague. Guess he's kinda doubtful, but no shit they found nothing when they searched me. First thing I did when that low-life got hit by the police van was to lose my coke. No fucking way am I going up on a charge of possession. Suppose they could ran a blood test, but thankfully they don't seem that interested in the fact I was wired. Still am, but I've had a couple of hours to straighten out a bit before they started this bullshit. I'm telling these guys the truth here - it was an accident. Self-defence. Just lucky it didn't happen in the States - I'd have shot that asshole myself.

"OK, tell it to us again, one more time from when you left the club."

This cop's a sorry looking son-of-a-bitch: about forty, overweight, bald, well-worn chain store suit. Just blends into the surroundings of this interview room. His colleague: she's younger, better dressed, never takes her eyes off me, fucking unsettling. I slug down a mouthful of their coffee, trying to ignore the grease floating on top. Anything to help stay focused and get out of here.

91

"Like I said, Harry and I were upstairs, having a quiet drink. I'd just been to the bathroom and when I got back to the table this manager guy's there, telling Harry we have to leave, like straightaway. There's been some problem downstairs. Claims Harry's guests have been dealing drugs. Harry objects, tells the guy where to get off, next thing he comes back with two doormen and they physically manhandle us out the door. I tell you, after you've finished here you should be down there arresting them for assault. They're lucky I don't press charges."

"Oh, we'll be interviewing all witnesses to events this evening Miss Sanders, you can be assured of that. Now just tell us how long you were in the bathroom for?"

That's this younger cop, the female black chick joining in now, virtually the first thing she's said all interview. Nasty measured tone to her voice as well.

"Couple minutes. I was just fixing my make-up."

She looks at the older guy who tells me to go on. Real goddamn double act these two.

"OK, so we get outside. Harry's pissed at these guys, tells Rio the driver to take him back to his flat then clear off."

The older cop asks why Harry was so upset at them.

"Because they were the reason we'd been thrown out. Turns out they'd gone into the bar and tried to deal drugs. Someone must have told security. I guess that explains why they carried them around in the car all the time."

"Maybe they also deal to passengers? There was evidence of drugs in the back seat."

This bitch's looking me straight in the eye as she asks this. So what, they've found nothing on me. I had nothing to do with Rio's death. I've had enough of this bullshit.

"Sure, maybe they do, but they didn't on this occasion."

Older guy asks me to carry on telling them what happened after we got thrown out of the bar.

"Like I said, Harry and this Rio guy were arguing. Rio was demanding money he said Harry owed, threatened him, then started threatening me. Not directly, just insinuated things. I was scared they'd try and you know, rape me or something."

"So just to be clear, are you accusing Mr. Rix and Mr. Millen of attempted rape, Miss Sanders?"

Look this bitch right in the eye as I answer her.

"I'm a woman. I felt in a vulnerable position. I didn't know what these guys were capable of, but no I'm not accusing them of attempted rape. Just saying I was afraid of them and their behaviour was becoming increasingly threatening. Do you want me to continue?"

Look at the older guy as I say this. He nods, so I go on.

"So Harry agrees to give them their money. We all get back in the car, drive to an ATM nearby. Harry pays Rio then Rio starts beating the shit out of him. Balbeck tried to defend Harry and next thing Rio's been hit by one of your police vans. It's like I said at the beginning, it was self-defence. These guys were threatening us and beating up our friend. I just wanted the whole nightmare to end. I never thought the evening would turn out like this."

I start sobbing now, saying that I'm really tired and just want to go home, which is true. Then someone else come in. Must be another cop. Speaks quietly to the female cop, guess she must be the one calling the shots here. She dismisses the cop who just came in.

"OK, apparently your story of what happened at the bar has been confirmed by the staff there. You're free to go now but we will need to talk to you again later. Make sure we're able to contact you, Miss Sanders."

I know they've got nothing on me. Just hope the others don't start blabbing about the drugs and stick to what Harry told us to say in the few seconds we had together back in the street before the police took control of the situation. It's like Harry said, it was self-defence, the guys were assaulting him and had threatened me. They'd been caught dealing drugs and were trying to get money from him. I mean, that's pretty much how it happened right? Billy's not exactly about to start telling the police about his little drug dealing sideline is he? Anyway even if he did, whose word are people gonna accept, that losers or ours? Balbeck's the one whose ass is in danger of getting slung in jail, but that's not really my problem, is it?

Harry Stanton

Fuck my faces hurts. Turns out the wound was pretty superficial; thank God my nose wasn't broken. Couple of stitches was all it needed but it still throbs like a bitch. Take a look at myself and wince. My eyes have swollen up and my nose is just a bloody mess. Fuck all chance of my getting laid this Christmas now unless I pay for it. At least I'm back home now at my London flat, can lie low here for a while. Fuck the business school. Term's over anyway.

I must have been released before the others. Fuck all case for me to answer really. That bastard assaulted me, end of story. I didn't ask Balbeck to start re-enacting some third rate Jean Claude Van-Damme movie. Told the police I didn't really see much. Rio assaulted me, the others obviously felt threatened and Balbeck lashed out. What happened afterwards was an accident. Even managed to get back the money that bastard had extorted from me. I guess the Police could have Balbeck on a manslaughter charge. Would be a shame, but what can I do about it? Simone and Danny should be clear providing they ditched the drugs. As for Billy, reckon he's fucked. The police will link him to all the drugs in the car and he'll be looking at a stretch at Her Majesty's pleasure. Couldn't happen to a nicer guy. Do I feel any guilt over that scumbag Rio's death? Absolutely none, thugs like him have it coming, it's always only a matter of time.

What time is it? Look at the alarm clock: just before 9am. No way I'm going to get any more sleep, even though I'm exhausted. Realise I don't have any of the others' mobile numbers so can't get in touch with them even if I wanted to. Suddenly I feel hungry, haven't eaten breakfast and the dinner last night seems like another lifetime. Go downstairs to the kitchen. Mark's gone to work already by the looks of things. Judging by the amount of scanty underwear draped over the radiators either Charmaine's moved in or Mark's into cross-dressing. Know who I'd rather see in a thong. Take a look in the fridge, sod all in there but Bacardi Breezers and nail varnish. Clearly Charmaine's skills don't lie in the kitchen. Decide to go back upstairs, get dressed and go get some food. Good old fry-up, just the thing in times of crisis like this. Get outside and it's bloody nasty. Sheets of rain are coming down. The weather matches my mood. By the time I get back from supermarket, I'm soaked. Decide to take a bath before cooking breakfast. So here I am, relaxing in the bath, trying to forget about last night. Start thinking about what Mark's getting up to with Charmaine under my roof, probably in this very bath, and suddenly my mind's on something other than the pain. Am in the middle of a momentary but pleasurable distraction when the phone rings. Shit, scramble out of the bath and wrap a towel round me. Still going to be embarrassing if I bump into Charmaine. Get to the phone before answer-machine picks up.

"Good morning, is it possible to speak with Harry Stanton please?"

Vaguely familiar voice, well spoken, slightly clipped accent, common in the City. Female as well, not so common in the City.

"This is Harry."

"It's Sarah Alcorn here Harry, Dean of the Business School. I need to speak with you urgently. I trust this is a convenient time."

94

Shit, she's obviously been informed about last night's little escapade, no doubt by the police. Play it cool see what she wants.

"Of course Dean, how can I help?"

"Well, I've been contacted by the police about last night's events. They've informed me that Balbeck Toyevski's being questioned in connection with the death of Rio Rix and that Billy Millen has been charged with supplying Class A drugs. I need to clarify the situation before an emergency meeting later this morning to assess the business school's position. Can you tell me everything you know?"

Shit, so Balbeck might be charged. That's rough but what the fuck does she mean, assess the business school's position? This has nothing to do with the fucking business school. None of this took place on campus; it wasn't a sanctioned outing. If Balbeck and Billy Millen get sent down, so what?

"I don't quite understand Dean. I thought this matter was being handled by the police?"

"The criminal aspects of it are, Harry, but I'm sure I don't need to remind you of the seriousness of the situation. One of our students is being held in custody pending a possible charge of involuntary manslaughter, one of our employees has been arrested for drug dealing, significant illegal drugs were found in the car in which you were travelling in last night and a young man who was in your company is dead. I've already had a lawyer claiming to represent Rio Rix's mother on the phone, threatening to sue the business school over this incident. Apparently, the booking for Mr. Rix's limousine was made in your name, giving the business school as your address. That very much involves us Harry. We've also had the local press on the telephone asking whether there's a drug problem amongst our students. It's only a matter of time before we have alumni and prospective students getting in contact expressing their concern. The global business school environment is highly competitive, the integrity of our reputation is of paramount importance. I cannot emphasise enough the concern that all of us here at the business school share over this unfortunate episode, Harry."

Sorely tempted to remind her that I wasn't responsible for admitting Balbeck Toyevski or employing Billy Millen, but resist. Sounds like I'm in enough shit as it is. I go through an edited version of the events of last night, making it clear I saw no drugs being dealt and the blame for this tragic episode lies squarely with Billy and Rio.

"Can I ask what part Simone Sanders played in all of these events, Harry?"

"Sure, Simone came along for the evening but that was it really. I think this Rio guy liked her, he kept making rude suggestions and that kind of thing. I think Simone was a bit scared of him, but she had nothing to do with his death."

"And what about Danny McMullen; I believe he was the other student?"

"Same thing. Danny was there, but he didn't do anything. He's a pretty quiet guy anyway, didn't really even notice he was there."

"OK, Harry thanks for your time. Unless there's anything else you'd like to tell me before I go?"

She leaves the question hanging in the air. I say there isn't and she ends by saying she'll want to talk to me back at the business school in the next day or so. Shit, I'd better get myself back up there and make sure the others have their stories straight. Think about Balbeck for a minute, but I'm sure his embassy and the business school will look after him.

Danny McMullen

Shit, dude, it's fucking miserable out here. Not wearing a watch so don't know exactly what time it is. I'd guess it's about 7am, hopefully the tube'll have started running, just need to get a train back home and crash. Asked about the others at the station and they told me Simone and Harry had already been released. Balbeck and Billy are still being held. That's heavy shit for Balbeck, if he gets charged with manslaughter he's gonna be thrown off the course, lose his scholarship, maybe end up in jail. Man, that's fucked up. Dunno what I can do to help him though. I guess he can get in touch with his embassy. Do they even have one? Must have a counsel or something. Maybe someone at the University can help him. Fuck, I wonder what they're gonna have to say about all this. At least they don't know about the drugs. Also doesn't look like I'm gonna be charged with anything. Nope, sounds like it's Balbeck who's the one really in the shit here.

Get on a bus, everyone's crammed in tight with the smell of damp clothes adding to the downbeat mood. The windows on the bus are all steamed up but someone tells me the tube station's just round the corner. Thankfully the bus stop's nearby, though I'm still soaking by the time I get there. Buy a ticket to King's Cross and get on the tube; people are looking at me kinda strange. I guess I do look a bit fucked up amongst all these early morning commuters. I haven't slept, I'm still wearing my dinner suit complete with bow tie, add in the comedown from the drugs and alcohol and I'm in a bit of a state. Mind you, looking around the carriage there're a few other people not looking much healthier. Managed to drag myself across London, catch the train and then hide myself behind a broadsheet newspaper that I'm way too distracted to read.

Keep thinking about Balbeck and that Rio guy. The dude's dead, fucking for real or what. When I finally make it back to my room, I shower then try to get some sleep. But I can't, keep seeing Rio's body crumpling as that police van hit him, the dull thud of the impact. Everything just kinda went blurred after that. Harry lurched over, telling us to ditch any drugs. I had that E tablet and some hashish left; just dropped them in a drain.

"It was self-defence, he was threatening us, stick to that and don't mention the drugs."

That's all Harry had time to say before the police were taking our names, asking us to come with them to the station. The rest of us were too shocked to say anything. Especially Balbeck, he just stood there staring at Rio's dead body with a real vacant look in his eyes. Didn't say anything when the police put him in the van. Harry had blood streaming down his face. Simone looked like she was about to faint. Billy was yelling though.

"He killed him, that bastard there, he killed Rio. They all saw it. He kicked him into the street in front of the van. It was murder, cold-blooded fucking murder."

Billy's pointing at Balbeck, almost choking with fury.

The police called for an ambulance for Rio, even though it was obvious he was dead. Then they sealed off the scene. Standing looking at Rio's dog licking his lifeless face, its tail curled in beneath its short legs, the realisation of what happened hit me. I felt like throwing up. All the champagne I drank felt like acid in my stomach. Thankfully we got to the police station pretty quick, where they took our details and searched us, before questioning us separately. I just told them what happened. Well, more or less, didn't mention the drugs and tried to paint it as favourably for Balbeck as I could. But there's no hiding it. He kicked the dude into the street and now the guy's dead. After a couple of hours they let me go. Now I'm just sitting in my room with my head in my hands when the phone rings.

"Hi Daddy, are you coming up to see me on Saturday like you promised? Can we go to the toy store to see Santa?"

It's Caitlin. I remember I'd said I'd go up and visit on Saturday. Spend the weekend there, take her out and buy her a Christmas present. Give it to Karen to pretend it's from Father Christmas. The sound of Caitlin's voice makes me wonder if that Rio guy had any kids. I start crying.

"What's wrong Daddy, don't you want to come to see me? Is that why you're crying?"

"No sweetheart, Daddy's just crying because he loves you so much and he's very happy to be coming to see you."

What do I tell a five-year-old? Daddy's crying because he's just seen a man get killed? Because his whole life is a car wreck, because he's a thirty-five-year-old man, living the life of a twenty-year-old? I manage to get my shit together to say good-bye to Caitlin, tell her I'll see her on Saturday. Just after I put the phone down it rings again, must be her again, checking I'm OK. A five-year-old checking on a thirty-five-year-old, pathetic. It isn't Caitlin though, it's the Dean.

"Danny, I need to speak with you in person about the events of last night. Everyone here at the business school is very concerned over what happened. Can you come over to my office immediately please."

It's an instruction, not a question. I agree to meet her in half-an-hour, put on some clean clothes and walk over there. Gives me some time to get my head straight before facing her. Decide I'd better hide my stash of weed, just in case someone gets the idea to search my room. Think of chucking it but there's the best part of an ounce of good gear there, so fuck that. Hide it in my car, it's on the way anyway. Weigh up my situation on the walk over to the Dean's office. I mean, it's not like the police have charged me with anything, so what's the worst she can do even if she does suspect I'm lying? As long as I stick to the story I've given the police I'll be OK, right?

So, I'm outside her office. The vibe amongst the staff is weird. They're trying to act normal around me but failing badly. I mean, acting normal for them means ignoring the students, not talking to them like they are with me today. When I came in the main building the receptionists were whispering to each other when they saw me. At least there are no classes today so there aren't many students around. Bumped into a couple on the way in, from the icy looks they give me, word obviously travels fast. We're gonna be seriously unpopular here after this little episode, particularly if the papers get a hold of this. Our fellow students here aren't gonna thank us for dragging the reputation of this business school through the mire and no mistake. Can't really blame them, invest a pile of cash and a year of your life in something and you don't want someone fucking with your return. I'm sitting outside her office killing time. Pick up one of the glossy brochures marketing next year's program, full of smiling faces and glowing testimonials. Shit, it's got Simone and Balbeck in it. Some dude's gonna be busy editing that, almost start giggling but manage to hold it together. Dean Alcorn's PA comes out to the corridor and says she's ready to see me now. Tell myself to just stay cool and my ass is covered.

"Danny, thank-you for coming in to see me. Please take a seat."

She remains seated behind her desk as she says this, doesn't get up to shake hands. The room is small but functional. There're a couple of pictures of her on the wall with people I recognise, British royalty. Others I don't who look like politicians or businessmen. Obviously this gig has its perks for her, no way she's gonna let a scandal involving a couple of her students screw that up.

"So Danny, I've just come off the phone with the police. They've charged Balbeck with manslaughter. He's being held until someone posts bail for him. Unfortunately as a business school we're not in a position to do so but I'm sure his embassy will be able to sort something out fairly quickly on his behalf. Billy Millen has been charged with possession of illegal drugs. He has of course been dismissed from his position here with immediate effect. The police say that they are not intending to pursue charges against Simone, Harry or yourself. I think you can all consider yourself very fortunate. We have a full meeting of the management committee of the business school tomorrow morning when we will be considering what if any further action we will be taking over this incident. In the meantime, please avoid making any comment to the press, there's already scurrilous stories doing the rounds on the internet that portray the business school in a very unfavourable light."

Just then her phone rings.

"OK, put him through please."

She raises a finger at me indicating she's gonna take this call. By the look on her face it's not one she's looking forward to.

"Good morning, Giles. I'm sure I know why you're calling and please rest assured we are doing everything we can here to deal with the issue swiftly and effectively...

No, I haven't seen that particular story on the Internet, although I am aware there have been some rumours circulating, most of which have absolutely no basis in truth. I can categorically assure you there is no drug ring being operated out of this business school, nor do our students frequent brothels and lap-dancing clubs on a regular basis. As for the suggestion that lecturers have been sleeping with students and inflating their grades, I'm afraid that's simply too farcical for words...

Yes, but Giles that episode of the brawl in the senior common room between two of our professors over the relative merits of

99

Naomi Kline versus Noreena Hertz was resolved months ago. If you remember, both were issued with a formal written warning. It has no bearing on the current situation and I can't understand why it's resurfaced. As for the donation from a convicted fraudster, we accepted that money in the belief he was a legitimate businessman. The funds have been earmarked for vital projects and we're not in a position to return them now...

No, I accept that some of our rivals may well be revelling in our discomfort but to accuse them of starting these rumours without evidence is not something I can allow, Giles. Please remember your responsibility as head of our alumni association before making those kind of accusations...

Yes, I understand that Giles. Please believe me when I tell you that I share the concern of the alumni association entirely...

We are considering all possibilities Giles, but it is not a simple matter of expelling the students concerned in order to set an example. Technically, they have not been found guilty of any wrongdoing. We do have a responsibility to these students as well as the wider student body, and of course as you correctly point out the alumni, as so effectively represented by you."

What the fuck is this shit! Who the fuck is this dude trying to get us expelled? The police aren't charging us, how the fuck do they think they can get away with pulling this shit? Man, there's no way Simone or Harry'll accept this bullshit. The Dean can see I'm freaked out. She puts her hand up to indicate for me to keep my mouth shut while she finishes off this call.

"OK Giles, and yes I will be sending out an e-mail this afternoon to all the students and alumni assuring them of how seriously we are taking this matter and any suggestions of an attack on the business school's integrity."

She comes off the phone to this asshole, then turns her attention to me.

"OK Danny, thank-you for your patience. Now is there anything you wanted to tell me that you didn't mention on the phone earlier, anything at all? I'd strongly advise you to be honest with me here, Danny. I hope you accept I'm on your side here, however it's imperative I get to the truth of the matter in order to decide upon the correct course of action."

"No Dean, it's like I told the police and said to you earlier, we were just in the wrong place at the wrong time. I can't believe the business school would expel us when we've done nothing wrong."

"No decision has been taken to expel you yet, Danny. We will consider all aspects of this situation fully when we meet tomorrow morning. Now, if there's nothing more you want to tell me then that will be all. I'll speak to you again tomorrow afternoon after the board meeting."

She dismisses me with a curt nod. I shuffle out the door, my mind going haywire over the prospect of expulsion and what it could mean. Would I lose my job? Could they boot me out of the UK? Would it affect access to Caitlin? All these crazy thoughts are just pounding in my head. I know I've fucked up a lot in the past but please God not this. On the way out I pass Simone in the corridor, obviously waiting to go in. Dude, how did she manage to clean up like that when I still look like shit? She sees me but pretty much blanks me. Man, I hope she keeps her shit together in there.

Simone Sanders

Soon as I get out of that damn police station I hail a cab. No way am I putzing around on the subway. Need to get back home, shower, change and put this whole sorry episode behind me. The police seem to have bought the story, which was more or less the truth anyway. I should be home free, long as the others don't cough up about the drug use, but why should they? Wouldn't exactly portray them in a favourable light, would it?

"You look like you've had a good night out then sweetheart."

"Huh? Oh right, yeah I have. Just been catching up with some old friends."

Oh God, why am I talking to this guy? Don't encourage him.

"Time of year ain't it. So where you from, the States?"

"Yep."

"Whereabouts then? I got cousins in Florida, go over every couple of years, love it I do. Great weather, good food an'all. Love to move over there I would, but the missus won't have it. Too much of a homebird, what can you do, eh? Mind you, I love this country, proud to be English too I am, see that flag?"

He's pointing at some red cross on a white background hanging from his rear-view mirror. Seen it on the soccer shirts a couple of those cute guys wear. Who is it, David Owen or something? Too good-looking to be British.

"mmh..."

"Greatest flag in the world that is. 'Course don't get me wrong, I ain't got nothing against Americans and that coming over here, same culture ain't it? Just not all those foreigners. Not being racist, but they ain't English. So why you doing over here then, you a working girl?"

Hang on what's the guy saying on the radio, the police have interviewed four students from…

"Shut the fuck up would you!"

…can't hear it properly, tell him to turn the radio up but he's pulling over to the side of the road. Something about one of the students being charged with manslaughter and drugs being found at the scene.

"Who the fuck do you think you are, talking to me like that in my own cab? Sod off out of it then."

"Hey, come on I was only trying to listen to something important on the radio. I'm sorry I swore at you. Don't be such a hard-ass about it."

"Don't matter, you can sling your hook. This is my cab and I don't take abuse from no-one, least of all the likes of you."

"What'do you mean the likes of me?"

"It's bleeding obvious ain't it. You're on the game. Look at the state of you, cottoned on to it the minute I picked you up. Now go on, clear off out of it."

Then the sonofabitch, who's out of the cab by now, leans a tattooed forearm in trying to grab me and throw me out. Screw that.

"Take your grubby hands off me, I'm leaving. Florida's the right place for an asshole like you. Know why your wife won't go with you? 'Cause she's screwing around over here. While you're out driving this piece of shit, she's at home getting banged up the ass by some foreigner. Probably right as we speak."

I'm out of the cab and off down the street as I say this, leaving him standing there hurling abuse. Thankfully, it's still early morning and there's plenty of other cabs around. Next guy's not a conversationalist, suits me. I'm back at King's Cross in no time and there's a train all set to go. Grab a Starbucks and find the emptiest carriage, not in the mood to have some asshole start hitting on me.

It's about 8:30am by the time I get back to my apartment. Feel like shit to be honest. Take a shower, check my phone messages: there's one.

"Hi darling, it's Mom. Hope you're well. Dad and I have been thinking about you. We'd love for you to come and visit this Christmas. We know you're real busy over there, but it'd just be so good to see you. Aunt Bonnie and the kids are coming over, they'd love to see you, too. Your cousin Monica's bringing her little girl Buffy over, she's six months old now. I'm sure Buffy would love to see her auntie Simone."

Buffy can shit in her diapers for all her auntie Simone cares.

102

"Anyway, darling, I hope you're not working too hard and getting too stressed. You know that isn't good for you. We all love you and miss you, and we're all real proud of you."

Yeah, well, whatever, hit the delete button and go to bed.

I'm in that twilight zone of kinda sleeping and kinda not when the phone goes again. Tempted to just let it ring, but it might be the police or another hedge fund wanting to talk to me. Turns out it's the Dean, she informs me my presence is requested in her office in about half an hour. Could really do without this but I guess she's gotta go through the motions of making sure we're OK, hasn't she?

So here I am, cleaned up, sobered up, outside her office. That jealous queen Matt who works for her has told me to wait outside. Had a couple of run-ins with him in the past. I mean, I'm a customer here, I expect the Dean to be accessible when I need to see her, not hide behind some disco bunny. I'll be telling him that before I leave this place as well, believe me. Then the door opens and out comes Danny. Looks like he wants to speak to me, but I've had quite enough of his company for one lifetime. Thankfully, Matt tells me the Dean's ready for me now in that prissy, self-important manner of his, whatever.

"Simone, thank-you for coming to see me. Sit down please."

I try to speak but she raises her hand. OK so this is her show, let's hear what she has to say.

"As I've just explained to Danny, the police are not at present intending to press charges against Danny, Harry or yourself. However, Balbeck has been charged with involuntary manslaughter and Billy with possession of drugs with intent to supply. I am sure you can appreciate the seriousness of situation for the business school. The management committee will be meeting tomorrow morning to discuss the situation and identify how we can move forward from here. Now, is there anything you'd like to tell me relating to your involvement in the events of the past twenty-four hours?"

"Only that it's been a horrendous experience for me Dean, as I'm sure you can appreciate. Also, I'm afraid I have to express just how disappointed I am in the business school here and I do expect some form of compensation, which no doubt will reflect the extent of the personal distress I have suffered."

"You what?"

She looks stunned by this and momentarily loses her poise. Well, there are rumours she's actually from quite a modest background. In fairness, she quickly recovers herself and raises herself up in her seat, taking her glasses off and putting both palms flat on the table.

"Excuse me Simone, I'm sure I must have misunderstood you. Just to clarify, you are telling me that you expect the business school to compensate you for becoming involved in an incident which has led to the death of a young man, a fellow student being charged with manslaughter and an employee being arrested for drug dealing, who incidentally is now claiming rampant drug use at this business school? That is before we even consider the raft of unfavourable publicity and scurrilous rumours circulating on the Internet, which are potentially ruinous to our reputation as one of this country's finest educational establishments."

"Indeed Dean, and if I may state the obvious, you have just explained exactly why I will be seeking compensation. I signed up for this MBA confident in the knowledge that I would be receiving one of the finest business school educations money could buy. Instead, I find that your admission's body has been so lax it has admitted a student who kicks a man to his death in a street, and your employment practices include hiring a drug pusher and then facilitating his dealing to young and vulnerable individuals here at the school."

Boy is she looking pissed now. I reckon all these rich dignitaries pictured on the wall with their beaming smiles never got to see this side of her when they were pressing palms.

"Well, if I may also, as you put it, state the obvious, you were, now what's the expression, off your head, at the dinner last night Simone. Your behaviour was crass in the extreme and I must say widely noted by your student peers."

The bitch's trying to sound all senatorial but she's not looking quite so confident now.

"I readily admit I had a glass or two of champagne. Like I said last night, I don't usually drink so it may have got me a little tipsy. However I would refute any accusations of drug abuse entirely if indeed that is what you are implying Dean, which I'm sure it isn't. To make this type of accusations against one of your students without any hard evidence would, I'm sure you'll agree, be a very reckless act."

That's trumped her. She's speechless with rage but there's jack shit she can do and she knows it. Maybe I'll let her save a little dignity, put some credit in the bank.

"Look Dean, I have the upmost respect for you and the ideals of this school. This has been a very trying episode for us all and of course we need to give our support to our colleague Balbeck at this difficult time. Maybe we should all concentrate on that and accept that the police have done their job with regard to myself, Harry and Danny. In short Dean, I feel we need to draw together as a community - not fall apart. Wouldn't you agree? Now if you don't mind, Dean, I'm totally exhausted and really need to get some sleep. After all I've got exams to prepare for next month, haven't I?"

She's beat and she knows it. A minute later I'm out the door, smiling graciously at Matt, who looks like someone's just peed in his Cheerios. Bet he reckoned I'd come crawling out of here. Yeah? Well, he bet wrong.

Harry Stanton

"Harry, it's Marianna, are you OK? I heard what happened. It's terrible. Everyone here is so shocked, there are some terrible stories going around, about drugs and guns and that Balbeck is going to prison. They aren't true are they?"

Fuck's sake, this is getting well out of hand.

"I'm fine Marianna, little shaken up. It was a rough night. Listen babe, don't believe everything you hear. There were no guns and no drugs, not that I saw anyway. It was an accident really."

"How about Balbeck, is it true he's in jail?"

"I think the police wanted to ask him some more questions about what happened. I'm sure he'll be fine, he didn't mean for anyone to get killed."

I'm on the train when I say this, a little too loudly, and a couple of people are looking at me pretty suspiciously. Can't say as I blame them really, guy with a smashed up face talking about death, drugs and guns, must look well dodgy. One guy's trying to hide behind his Daily Telegraph but can't resist taking a peek at me, couple of younger girls are also looking over but with a little more interest than distaste. Right now, however, even my libido's at a pretty low ebb.

"I hope so. Listen Harry, I'm glad you're safe. I sort of feel guilty that I didn't come with you last night. Maybe none of this would have happened if I'd been there. You don't blame me, do you?"

"Christ no. Look, none of this is your fault Marianna, things just got a little out of control. Listen, I'm on my way back to school now, everything will be fine."

"Promise you'll call me if you need anything, OK?"

"Of course babe, and Marianna, thanks for calling, bye."

She rings off and I'm left wondering just how bad this is for me. I mean, the police haven't charged me with anything, and they're not going to either. Not least because I didn't actually do anything.

Sure, it's going to give everyone something to talk about for a few days, but really the only one who stands to lose anything, apart from Rio and Billy of course and they don't count, is Balbeck, who frankly stands to lose just about everything. Once I get back to my place and get sorted out I'll phone the police and check what's happening with him. Only fair, suppose he was trying to help me when it happened.

An hour later I'm back home, trying fruitlessly to catch up on some course reading. There's a ring on the buzzer. Shit, I hope this isn't the police.

"Harry boy, it's Sean. Let me in then, I'm freezing my bollocks off down here."

It's big Sean, just what the doctor ordered, a bit of civilized company. Maybe chat this situation through over a couple of pints, numb the pain of my face a bit. He clumps up the stairs, usual uniform of blue jeans, football shirt and black leather jacket, not exactly a fashion victim our Sean. Still it's good to see him.

"Fancy a pint then, Sean?"

"Does the pope wear a silly hat?"

Take that as a yes and off we go to the Castle. Sean swears by the Guinness in there so that's fair enough by me. We say little on the short walk there, but there's something hanging in the air, couple of pints of the black stuff will bring it all out though. Usually does. Sean grabs a booth in the far corner, I order the pints from the barmaid, a moderately fit young Eastern European who's clearly been employed for her arse rather than her ability to pour a decent pint of Guinness. He grimaces a bit when I set the still settling pints of Guinness down.

"Jesus, is there nowhere in this town you can get a decent pint of stout nowadays?"

I just grin, it's not a question.

"So what the fuck was the crack last night then?"

"Fuck knows, it all just got a bit out of hand Sean. The guy driving and his mate who works in the kitchen, God knows what he was doing there, anyway they turned out to be a pair of fucking psychos. Drove us down to London then followed us into my club and started dealing drugs. Ended up with us all getting chucked out. Then they start demanding money from me, when I pay up the big bastard driving fucking head-butts me. Look at the state of this."

"Nasty all-right, but I guess he paid for it. Wouldn't have had your man Balbeck down for a killer, right enough."

"Me neither but fuck me, I didn't ask him to do it. Just came out of nowhere. Chopped the bloke in the throat, then kicked him

106

in the chest, back into the street, straight into the path of a police van."

"Jesus wept, still reckon he might have saved you from an even bigger beating by the sound of it."

I grunt noncommittally, that's what's been on my mind ever since. Was Rio finished with me or just starting? And what about the others? He clearly had the horn for Simone, can't blame him there, but what was he going to do about it? I mean, she'd been giving him the come-on good and strong a bit earlier. What if that had turned nasty? Then again, maybe they'd just have taken the money and fucked off. I'd still have a sore face but shit happens.

"So where's Balbeck now then, still being held by the peelers?"

"Yep, I phoned when I got back. Said he's in front of the magistrate tomorrow morning, then I suppose the business school or his embassy will post bail."

"Harry, you're fucking having me on here. The business school aren't posting bail. Ma Alcorn's already washed her hands of it according to Siobhan in the admin office. As for his embassy, what fucking planet are you on? Do you know anything about Kyrgyzstan?"

"It's one of those former Soviet block states, like Ukraine or something?"

"Harry mate, it's a piss poor shithole in the middle of nowhere. Siobhan says they reckon bail will be about ten grand, the entire fucking Kyrgyzstan GDP is about ten grand. They may help get him a lawyer, but no way are they bailing him out. The poor bastard's up shit creek without a paddle."

"So what the fuck am I meant to do about it?"

"You just have a think about that while I get another round in, same again?"

I nod, I know what Sean's saying and I know why he's saying it. This guy helped you out, you owe him, end of story. The old Irish honour system. But hold on, I didn't ask him to. Ask me, by jumping in he made a bad situation worse. In fact, he shouldn't even have been there in the first place. I tell Sean this when he comes back. I also ask him where the fuck he was last night.

"You just hang on a minute there. I never said I was coming for definite. You arranged that trip because you wanted to get your leg over, which is the reason you do everything, Harry boy. You spend most of the time walking about like a dog with two dicks, and it fucks up your head. No way would you be getting involved with a headbanger like that Simone Sanders doll otherwise; she's bad news mate."

"C'mon Sean. She's not that bad. A bit of a handful maybe, but…"

He interrupts me, getting quite worked up which isn't like Sean. Usually takes life in his stride.

"She's twisted mate and I'm not just talking about the run-in I had with her earlier in term. You know wee Donna who works on reception?"

I nod, quite cute but quiet and young; pleasant girl actually.

"Well, one day Miss Sanders decides she need some photocopying done, obviously she's too busy herself like, so she tells Donna to do it. Donna says she'd like to help but she can't leave the phones unattended. So Simone screams at her, what the fuck does she mean she'd rather sit around waiting for her boyfriend to call than do the job she's paid for? Then tells her she pays more than twice as much in fees as Donna earns in a year, that the shoes she's wearing cost more than Donna's entire wardrobe, and that if she wants to keep her job she better get in there and do the photocopying right now or Simone will personally drag her up to the Dean's office. Harry mate, Donna's seventeen, this is her first job, poor kid was in tears all afternoon. Siobhan and the other girls had to take her out for a drink just to persuade her to stay on."

"Yeah, but did she do the photocopying?"

Realise that was a bad joke soon as I've said it and say so. Tell Sean I'm just stressed out with everything that's happened over the past twenty-four hours.

"No problem, just trying to point out a few home truths to you mate. People like you Harry, but sometimes you can be a right cunt."

There, that's me told. We both start laughing. The atmosphere lightens, Sean drains his pint and stands up.

"Yeah, she did the photocopying for her, been doing mine all term as well, happy days."

I finish up and we leave the bar, going our separate ways at the door after shaking hands. Guess I need to decide what to do about Balbeck, better speak to Simone and Danny. After all, they're involved in this too.

Balbeck Toyevski

This police station reminds you of the university in Bishkek. It is grey, cold and functional. Even the smell of disinfectant in the police cell is familiar. The bench you have been sitting on for many hours is hard but that does not matter, there was never any chance

108

that you would sleep. A tray of food they left earlier is sitting there cold and uneaten. Things have turned out very badly and you are in a lot of trouble. Maybe the police will talk to you again, although they have already spoken to you several times but you told them very little, because there is very little to tell. Do not punish yourself too much, after all you did not mean to kill that man, only to stop him hurting Harry. Also, you were concerned that he would hurt Simone. She was very afraid of him. You were not afraid of him though. In Krygyzstan you learned kick-boxing. Uncle taught it to you as a young boy.

"Come Balbeck, you are the man of the house so you must learn to fight like a man. Box me now and do not cry like a baby if your nose is bloody."

He used to get on his knees in the kitchen so he was the same height as you when you were seven years old, then he would put on an old pair of boxing gloves and teach you to box. Later he took you outside and taught you to kick.

"Show me an axe-kick boy. Not like that, you kick like a girl. Kick like a man, like this."

Many times your nose was bloody from his punches, and shins sore from him blocking your kicks, but always you learned more. Then one day his nose was bloody and his shins sore and he started to box little brother instead. As you got older you were too busy studying to have time to box, but at the university in Bishkek there was a kick-boxing club, so sometimes you would train there. Tamara did not like kick-boxing though, she was afraid that you would get hurt.

You never thought there would be a need to use the things that Uncle taught. In Kyrgyzstan, people do not fight in the street like they do in England. Maybe it would be better if Uncle had not taught you to box, then you would not have kicked the driver of the car into the street and caused his death. But there is no point thinking like that. What is done is done.

So what will happen now? The embassy have given you a lawyer here but what can she do? It is very simple what happened last night. You have explained it to the police and now there is nothing more to be said. The lawyer has tried to explain how the law works in England, but you are confused. It seems that tomorrow you go to the court and then someone has to pay money before they release you, then later they arrest you again before being put on trial. The lawyer said she will try to speak to some people to raise the money so you do not have to stay in jail before the trial, but what does that matter? It is not jail you are afraid of, but the shame and dishonour that you have brought on Tamara and the family. You have killed a man, so now you must wait here and accept you will be punished for your crime. Whatever happens, I know you will face up to your responsibilities like a man and do what must be done.

Danny McMullen

No shit, just sitting here in my bedroom looking at some of these stories about the business school doing the rounds on the Internet. Heavy stuff, man. There's one here claiming the MBA students import cocaine directly from Columbia, then sell it on to the undergraduates at a hefty mark-up. Another says we're behind a chain of massage parlours in university cities throughout the UK, whilst this one accuses our Russian students of using the hefty tuition fees as a form of money laundering. Apparently two dudes from Moscow turned up beginning of the year having paid their fees in cash, then split after two weeks saying they didn't like the course and demanded their money back. Pretty smart, that one actually. Not that I remember seeing them. Man, who makes all this shit up? Must be students from other business schools. I guess they're competing for the same prize: that job at McKinsey or Goldman Sachs or wherever. Our little escapade just gave them the ammunition they needed to bad-mouth us. Perfect, as if things weren't tough enough here, now I gotta deal with a hundred pissed-off classmates. There's already a chain of furious e-mails doing the rounds, general tone, needless to say, is not entirely sympathetic to us. Phone goes, fuck man, bet that's the Dean calling to expel me. Don't wanna answer it, but I better.

"Danny, Hi. Listen, it's Harry. We need to talk."

"You think? I mean, the Dean's probably made her mind up already what to do about us."

"No, it's about Balbeck. He's in deep shit, they're charging him with manslaughter."

"Yeah, I heard, but what can we do?"

"We can bail him out. There's no-one else. The University and his government won't, which just leaves us."

Shit, that's tough on the dude. Harry's right, but this is gonna cost.

"I suppose, but Harry, like just how much money we talking here?"

"His lawyer reckons it'll be about ten grand. It's only bail money. We get it back when he goes to trial in about a month."

Ten grand, shit I only got a couple of grand left to do me 'til the end of the course. No way can I get my hands on that kinda dough.

"Sorry man, I'll do what I can but I just ain't got that kinda cash at the minute. What about Simone?"

"Tried her, she told me to fuck off. Said she wants nothing more to do with us ever again. Says she's going to sue any students circulating allegations she took drugs last night."

That figures. Still, Harry's got plenty of cash. Can't he cover the ten grand if it's only for a couple of weeks? Says he can but he thinks I should help.

"Danny, I'm fucking hacked off at this whole thing. You think I need this crap right now? But fuck knows what those guys would've done if it hadn't been for Balbeck. We can't just leave him hanging out to dry. You gonna help out or not? We need to decide now or he'll spend the weekend in jail."

"OK, OK, look I can let you have two grand. That's it, sorry man, I ain't got any more."

"Fine, alright, better than nothing. The bail hearing's in the morning. I'll get down there then and hopefully bring him back up here so we can start to sort all this shit out."

"What about the Dean? Think she'll expel us?"

"Doubt it, we didn't break any laws. The police aren't charging us, what grounds has she to expel us? She's just trying to scare us a bit. We're not fucking eighteen years old. It's bullshit."

"Yeah, I guess. She did seem pretty pissed this morning though."

"Yeah? Well, she hasn't even asked to see me yet. Forget about it, we're not getting expelled."

Harry says he's gotta run. He'll come up with the cash tomorrow then I'll give him my share afterwards. After we hang up, I take a long hot shower and think about what he said. Makes sense. Anyway, as long as I get the money back when Balbeck goes to trial then that's cool. Decide I'll still go to Manchester this weekend to see Caitlin, whatever happens. No point sweating it too much. Still, a heavy fucking gig though. Poor Balbeck, having to spend another night in the cells. Wonder if anyone's said anything to his family?

No way, can you believe the nerve of this guy? He's gotta be kidding. Come on!

"Harry, let me make myself perfectly clear. I'm not paying one red cent to get that idiot released. You created this mess Harry, you can deal with it, period."

"But you were there, you saw what happened. Come on, Simone. He needs us. If we don't help him, who will?"

"Tough shit, I'm the innocent victim here. My reputation is getting shot to fuck and none of this is my fault. People are making all kinds of accusations about me, my picture's all over the Internet, and now you're coming on the phone asking for money? You gotta be fucking kidding me?"

Finally, he gets the message. Don't think Harry's gonna be wanting to jump my bones in the future but you know what? I can live with that. That's the one good thing to come outta last night: the fact I didn't put out for that schmuck. It's mid-afternoon now and I'm sitting in my living room, feeling pretty wiped out after everything that's happened. Just need to get my head straight. Decide I'll go for a run just to try and kick-start my system back to life. Sweat out some of those toxins from last night too. Take a good look at myself in the full length mirror in the bedroom when I'm changing into my running gear. Still like what I see, but gotta watch it now I'm getting older. Anything goes on my ass now isn't gonna be easy to shift.

Outside, it's cold but dry. Good day to pound the pavement. I take a left out of my apartment block and run towards the river. It's about a mile away and I'm making good time. Decide to run along the river bank for a couple of miles, it's peaceful here. I'm feeling pissed at Harry for getting me involved in this fucked up situation in the first place. Running hard helps me vent my frustration at him and all those other idiots whispering about me behind my back. If I've got something to say to someone, I say it to their face, not like these gutless backstabbers who'll be sitting around spreading their poison about me. Run past the spot where we dumped the dogs' bodies, seems like that was a lot longer than only two months ago. Suppose I shouldn't have killed them, really. Guess I just wasn't thinking straight. Anyway, if anyone's to blame it's the authorities here, not me. Shouldn't have forced my hand. Like I wasn't under enough pressure already? I'm running hard, really working my muscles, my lungs are taking in the icy English air. It's starting to get dark, I've been running for quite a long time now but I don't feel like stopping. I'm back on the pavement now and I run past a car stopped at traffic lights with a baby seated on a woman's lap in the back. The car pulls off and I'm running parallel with the baby for a few seconds, even though it's dark I can tell it's looking at me and smiling. I start to think about Patrick and our unborn baby. Why he let me down, when he said he wouldn't leave Tammi.

"This isn't just about us, Simone. Tammi needs me. I can't leave her, can't turn my life upside down just to be with you. You've always known that."

What about me? What about my carrying a man I love's baby who doesn't even want me? What does that do to my life? I knew then Patrick had made his decision and what that decision meant. It was a year ago today I had the abortion. I remember staring up at the sky for I don't know how long before I walked into the clinic. There wasn't a cloud in it. Then sitting in the waiting room on my own, blanking out the offers of counselling posted on the pale blue walls. Knowing that any minute the door would open and they'd call my name. Then ask if anyone was with me. Patrick had tried to insist on coming. I couldn't handle the thought of that. Dealing with his anxiety, the pretence that he was there for me failing to mask his desperation that I go through with "it".

What was "it", Patrick? Why couldn't you even speak about this thing you were asking me to do?

"It's tough, but it's the only rational solution, Simone."

Tough. Rational. You repeated these words like they were a mantra, Patrick. Like I didn't know what it would mean trying to bring a kid up on my own. The inevitable haemorrhaging of the promises I'd made to myself. I'd seen it at work: women getting marginalised, written off. And the men who'd start sniffing round me. Their egos boosted by my situation. So in the end I let them strap me to a bed and put a vacuum cleaner between my legs. It was easier.

And no, I didn't need you to come with me Patrick. Didn't need you to help me walk back to my car. To distract my attention from the protesters at the gate, calling me a murderer. I managed just fine without you.

Despite running harder, it's still cold. I can feel the tears freezing on my cheeks. I know I should turn back now but I just feel the need to keep going. I remember how afterwards I tried to avoid people, even though no-one knew anything other than Patrick. Even Hamilton didn't know about the abortion, despite us still living together. I'd be at a party or social function and sure on the surface I'd seem fine but people talking around the room, none of them would realise the state I was in. If they did they'd only have blamed me. For trying to wreck a marriage, for having an abortion, for cheating on my boyfriend. Sure there was plenty to blame me for, no denying it. Of course I couldn't keep working with Patrick. I mean I tried, but it was impossible. Especially if he tried to be kind to me. Was so different when we were screwing. Then he called me his tethered goat. Loved to put me in front of clients, especially the nerds. Said he got off on watching them watching me. In the office it had been a game to Patrick, hiding what we had. Dropping just enough little hints to live a bit dangerously. Enjoying the attention that comes with speculation. Not any more. He became skittish around me.

"We've got to maintain our professionalism, Simone. You can't keep following me around like this. Promise me you'll take some time off work if it all gets too much."

We were alone in the lift when he was whispering this. He'd taken his glasses off and was leaning forward into my face. Was wearing a different aftershave. Something less musty than the one I liked, more clinical. His shirt, too, was different. White with a button down collar. Single cuff, worn with a yellow tie. He looked somehow less imposing, like he'd been stripped of some of his masculinity. Suddenly felt sorry for him.

"Patrick, is this what you're settling for?"

"What?"

"This y'know...mediocrity?"

"Stop it Simone. Get a grip, please."

The urgency in his voice was increasing as the lift stopped and he snatched my hand away from his face before the doors opened. A couple of suited back office nobodies got in but Patrick starts shooting the breeze with them like they were all part of the same deal team. These guys weren't as dumb as they looked though. Caught them looking at me looking at him. As for Patrick, all I saw now was regret in his eyes where there used to be desire. Anything else I could handle, but not that. I quit the next day.

I'm coming over the bridge now, there's a kid on a bicycle riding past me, looks about eighteen. I look at his satchel, it's got an American flag on it. He must be an exchange student or something. I remember when I was that age, when I started at Stanford and my Dad drove me there. We were happy. One night we stopped to stay over at a Motel 8 or some other Godawful cheap stayover in nowheresville Nevada. We'd been driving for four days solid, breaking the journey to stay in cheap motels, sharing a bedroom to keep the cost down. This one night there was a disturbance in the room next door, the couple were fighting real bad, sounded like the guy was beating up on her. Must have been a couple of kids in there too 'cause we heard them crying. My Dad went round there and spoke to the guy. I was scared, this asshole sounded like real white trash and mean with it, but whatever my Dad said we never heard any more yelling that night. I was proud of him then, probably for the last time. Never told him though. I knew he was proud of me even though he was worried about the tuition fees and everything.

"Simone, you can achieve anything you want in life, but you'll always be my little girl and I love you very much. Remember that."

We'd stopped at a diner the next morning when he told me this, but I remember I felt loved, appreciated. His eyes misted over and he took my hand and held it for the longest time. We were eating ice cream sundaes. Back then I didn't have to be so careful about what I ate. I'd forgotten about it, but now the memory comes back, unprompted. I never told them about the abortion but sometimes it's almost like they know anyway. I guess when I came back home from San Francisco it was obvious even to them something was up. Like how when they look at me now it's almost with pity rather than pride. Something I can never understand. What more could I have done to make them proud of me? To be a good daughter? Working the graveyard shift at the local Denny's during college summer break, so I wouldn't have to bum cash from them. Dealing with the drunks who pitched up after dollar drink night at the bars, red faced and leering at the waitresses, then not tipping more than a lousy dollar. Flipping the tablemats to the side showing cups of steaming coffee and glasses of orange juice, hoping we could get enough inside them so they could drive home in a straight line and not mow down some hardworking security guard or cab driver. Then at the end of the shift, cleaning up the stations. Making sure each table had exactly sixteen sugars, eight Equals and eight Sweet'n'Lows. Shitty work but I did it. Told them it was so I could pay my own way. Maybe so, or maybe I just felt more at ease in the company of drunks and minimum wage single mothers than I did with my own parents. Anyways, working there I stayed busy and that's what's kept me going all these years. All these years since my little brother died.When I saw him lying there in the road. I was only seven but I knew he was dead. I stayed with him. Just knelt there in the middle of the road. I knew it was the middle of the road because his body was stretched out horizontally across the white line. Kinda making the shape of a cross. Think there were other people there but I don't remember. Don't remember anything until my mother turned up. We both knelt by his body

115

together then she took me inside where we waited for my father. Asked my mother if we should pray that he'd come home and bring Nicholas with him? She didn't answer. I never prayed again after that night when my father came home alone.

It's now pitch black and I'm running back along the other river bank. There's a few people out walking dogs, couple of crews out rowing. A drunken hum comes from one of the pubs on the riverbank. I just keep running and running.

Chapter Ten

Harry Stanton

So I'm here in court. Sure enough, like his brief said, the bail is granted and posted at ten grand, which I agree to stump up. Balbeck doesn't seem that excited by the prospect of getting released. In fact, he looks like death warmed up, which under the circumstances shouldn't really come as any surprise. Better get him out of here and back up to the business school. Had a call from the Dean last night.

"Harry, I appreciate the responsibility you're displaying in this situation. Obviously I'll need to speak with Balbeck as a matter of urgency when he returns."

"Yeah, of course. I mean what's going to happen to him though?"

"I'm afraid I'm not at liberty to discuss that with you, Harry. We have to take the necessary action to protect the school's reputation. We owe that to all our students."

"What about Balbeck, surely you bear some responsibility for his welfare too?"

"Indeed, we readily acknowledge that. However I don't really think you're in a position to lecture me on responsibility Harry, do you?"

Fair point I guess. Anyway, we get the legal formalities over and done with in about half an hour and then Balbeck gets released. As well as the money, the other bail conditions require him to report to the local police twice daily and he's under a 10pm to 7am curfew. Not that I imagine he's in the mood for much partying given the turn of events. Poor guy looks completely shot to fuck. He's still wearing that dinner suit from Wednesday night. His solicitor has a quick word with him outside the court. Sounds like they're talking in Russian or maybe it's Kyrgyz, his embassy must have sorted this out for him. Pretty sure Kyrgyz-speaking briefs are thin on the ground in West London. Their discussion actually turns quite animated, but that changes on the way to the car with me when he says little. I mean, I don't expect him to be full of the joys of Spring but a little gratitude wouldn't go amiss.

"Look mate, we can nip back to my place if you want to have a shower and change of clothes. You can borrow a few of mine. We're about the same size. Sound good?"

"No, thank-you, I am fine as I am."

"Fair enough. Well, how about something to eat then? Can't imagine the grub was up to much in there."

He just grunts what I take to be a negative response. Suit yourself, looks like I'll be spending the next couple of hours listening to radio Talksport. Give it one more go.

"So what have you told people back home then, they must be pretty freaked out?"

"Nothing, nobody must know my shame."

"First of all mate, it was an accident. You didn't mean to kill him, and anyway he was a nasty piece of work. Secondly, how the fuck are you going to keep it from them? It's a non-starter."

Another grunt. Fuck, he's not exactly helping his own cause here. Decide to try and lighten the mood a bit.

"Listen, we'll all go to court and tell them what happened. They'll probably give you a suspended sentence or something, just send you back home. Worst case, you'll get a couple of years in a low security prison, behave yourself and you'll be out in no time."

"I will never be able to complete the course now, I have failed everyone."

"So what? Fuck that, even if they do kick you out it's only a poxy course. Couple of years this'll all be behind you. What age are you, twenty-six, twenty-seven?"

"Twenty-eight."

"Well, see what I mean? You're still young, fuck the course. Look, it's the other side of the world. No-one needs to know you've been in jail here. Just go back home, start again."

He turns and looks me right in the eye and shakes his head.

"You do not understand Harry, it is different for me. This was my great chance in life and I have wasted it."

Then he looks away, tilts back his head and closes his eyes. I guess this conversation is over and he's right, I don't fucking understand. The rest of the journey is spent in relative silence with only the radio discussion about England's lack of left-sided midfield options for company.

We get back and I drop him off at his digs, he smiles for the first time but it's a sad resigned smile.

"Thank-you Harry, it was good of you to help me today."

"It's OK. Look, thanks for what you did the other night. That guy might have seriously hurt me. I feel a bit guilty you got caught up in that, but like I said it was an accident, no way will the court see it any different."

He stares at me with a look of resignation in his eyes and puts his hand on my shoulder.

"Do not feel guilty, Harry. I must take responsibility for my own actions. I am not a child."

With that he shakes my hand and gets out, walking into his accommodation block without looking back. I drive away feeling a bit uneasy, but what more can I do? I'll call the Dean and let her know he's back. It's her fucking job to deal with this, not mine.

Balbeck Toyevski

The lawyer was trying to tell you to ask the Kyrgyz ambassador to intervene on your behalf, but she does not understand that you cannot do that. You know that you have created this situation by your own foolish actions: going out and getting drunk and pretending to be a person that you are not just to try to impress people. All that matters now is trying to protect the family's honour. Will you be able to go home and ask Tamara to marry you now? Do you think you still deserve her? Harry does not understand, he thinks you are scared to go to jail but you are not. It is important that he does not blame himself for what happens to you. It was right you took the chance to tell him that.

Now back in your room, sit down and write a letter to Tamara, explaining everything to her. It will be very difficult but try and be honest with her. You have known her since you were eighteen. She knows the kind of man you are. Remember when you first met? You were in the same class for economics and you always tried to sit close to her. You would show off in class, challenging the lecturers, letting everyone know how clever you were, but really you were just trying to impress Tamara. When you all went hiking in the mountains she let you carry her rucksack all the way to the top of Komsomolez mountain. You started at seven o'clock in the morning and the climb up took eight hours but with Tamara by your side you were too happy to be tired. When you reached the summit you sat and shared the tomato and cucumber with naan bread that Tamara had prepared. The air at the top of the mountain was cool and clear and you knew nothing in the world could compare with what you saw around you . No matter what happens now you must hold onto that memory, it is a good one. The telephone rings and you blink the tears from your eyes.

119

"Balbeck? Good morning Balbeck, this is Dean Alcorn. I would like you to come and see me in my office as soon as you can please. There are some things we need to discuss together in light of your current situation."

You will go and see her now before coming back and writing the letter to Tamara. You shower, change your clothes and polish your shoes before leaving the room, deciding to wear your suit to show proper respect for the Dean when you meet her.

You walk to her office through the town, it takes about 30 minutes. Today it is cold for England but so what, you know it is colder in Kyrgyzstan. At the business school there are several of your classmates gathered outside smoking cigarettes. Sometimes in Bishkek you used to smoke because you thought it made you look cool, but stopped because Tamara did not like it. Now, though, you would like a cigarette. You ask one of the girls if you may have one.

"Sure, of course you can Balbeck. Listen, we're all very sorry about what happened. It just sounds like a dreadful accident. I'm sure the court will take that into account."

You think her name is Jill, she is from England and speaks with a very nice accent, like how you imagined all British people talked before coming here. One of the guys, Leo his name is, offers his lighter to light the cigarette.

"Yeah mate, it's a bum deal but you've gotta just try and hang in there. What's your lawyer like, they any good?"

"She is trying to help me, yes, but I have to accept what has happened."

"Listen mate, I was a lawyer too, back in Oz. Not that familiar with the English legal system but they gotta take the circumstances into account, right?"

Leo is a good guy, remember at the beginning of term he was asking a lot of questions about Kyrgyzstan. He said he has travelled all through Central Asia but he has not been there. You were impressed that someone was interested in Kyrgyzstan when you heard this and invited him to come to visit Bishkek after you had all finished business school. You were keen to show off the new friends you had made to everyone back home. That will not happen now. Shrugging your shoulders, you can tell that they are all embarrassed and do not know what else to say. Everyone stands in silence for a minute while you quickly smoke the cigarette, before putting it out in the tall ashtray with sand outside. It was a Marlboro, very good cigarettes. Before going in, Jill smiles at you, a sad but kind smile, and Leo shakes your hand.

"Take it easy big guy, we're rooting for you."

As you go in, a couple of other students who you don't know, they must be research students, walk past. One of them nudges the other one and they look at you, ignoring them you go upstairs to the Dean's office. Her assistant asks you to wait outside her office and says that she will be free in a couple of minutes. One of the ladies from the administrative office of the MBA comes up to you. She stops and puts her hand on your arm and asks how you are doing. It is a very kind gesture, you smile and tell her things are OK. Then it is time to enter the Dean's office. This is the first time you have been in here. You would never have thought it would be for such a reason.

"Balbeck, sit down please. Now, I'd like you to tell me in your own words, exactly what happened on Wednesday evening."

You tell her what happened in the bar and how Harry got angry with the guy who was driving. How the guy threatened Harry and asked him for money. You could tell the driver was very angry and thought he might hurt Harry. After Harry gave him the money, the driver started to beat him. You could not allow this to happen to your friend so you punched and kicked the driver, but he fell into the street and was struck by a travelling police van. There is no question that you are to blame. You accept responsibility for his death entirely.

"OK, thank-you for being so candid with me. Now is this also what you have told the police?"

Yes, of course, this is what you have told the police. What else would she expect you to tell them?

"Balbeck, it's OK, I'm on your side. I'm just trying to get a clear understanding of the exact circumstances surrounding this unfortunate situation."

There is nothing left for you to say, she looks at you for a moment then she speaks.

"Balbeck you do understand that we want to help you, but we must also consider carefully the reputation of the business school and its obligations to our student and alumni bodies before deciding how to proceed in this matter?"

You nod, of course you understand this. Does she think you are stupid?

"Therefore, it is with great regret that I must suspend you from the MBA program until after your trial, which I believe will be in a few weeks time. Obviously we will reconsider the position after the court has determined the outcome of this case. Do you understand the implications of what I am telling you?"

Yes. You understand the implications of what has happened perfectly.

"OK, now as you know we have a counselling service available for students and Mrs Ferris, our counsellor, would like to speak with you in order that we can provide as much help and support for you as possible at this difficult time. Can you speak to her now?"

That will not be possible today. You have some things you must take care of for your family first.

"Surely you can spend ten minutes talking to her Balbeck? She is very experienced in dealing with all kinds of student problems."

You just shake your head and get up to leave.

You thank the Dean for her time and apologise for the trouble you have caused for her and the business school. She looks upset and embarassed but stands up and shakes your hand before you go.

"We will do what we can to support you, Balbeck."

You nod, then let go of her hand. Closing the door to her office, you leave the building quickly without stopping to speak to any of the other students. You know it is time now to take care of your affairs.

Danny McMullen

Slept real bad last night man. Kept going over what'd happened the night before. I know the guy was a low-life but whatever way you cut it, he's dead because of us. I mean, if Harry hadn't got so pissy with him, if Simone hadn't been such a prick-tease, if Balbeck had just stopped after he punched him in the throat when the guy was fucked anyway, he'd still be alive. But what about me? I went along for the ride, bought drugs from them, didn't step in when he attacked Harry. That's always been my problem, easily led. Just like Karen said when she dumped me.

"Don't just sit there and play the victim Danny, hiding away from the world and your responsibilities."

I just sat there and took it. Could've asked her how staying on in a crummy job I didn't want to do, in a country I didn't want to live in, to take care of her and Caitlin was hiding from my responsibilities. But I didn't. Just mumbled something about how I still loved her and we should stay together for Caitlin's sake. I still remember the look of contempt in her eyes when I said this. Knew for sure it was over between us then. It was different when she told me she was pregnant. She was nervous and uncertain then, just waiting for the inevitable let-down. I didn't let her down though and I never have, not where Caitlin's concerned. End of the day, that's why I'm here, trying to make myself into something I'm not.

So I see my daughter twice a month; try to be a father in the few lousy hours a month I'm allowed to spend with her. Even Karen knows that.

Enough of this self-pity crap, I need to get out of here and clear my head. I'm not hungry but I could use some coffee. Decide to go to the bank and get Harry's money. Stop in Starbucks on the way. There's a couple of other MBA's in there, looks like a study group. They've seen me and now they're looking my way. I go over.

"Hi guys, what's this, revision session or something?"

It's Decker Honeycutt, Brett Rusk and a couple of other A list, master-of-the-universe types.

"Actually, it's a private gathering Danny. We should have been attending a career's presentation from a group of venture capitalists, but they cancelled at the last minute. Then that shouldn't surprise you, should it?"

The rest of them nod at this comment from Hilary Jenkins-Spires, real English ice maiden. Then it's someone else's turn.

"Danny, I think I can speak for all of us here when I say that we don't presume to sit on judgement on you guys, but you've let our community down. What happened on Wednesday night reflects on all of us."

Fuck this.

"OK Brett, you know what, fuck you and the boat you sailed in on. A guy is dead, one of our classmates may lose everything. Do you give a shit about that or do you just care how this all looks on your resume?"

"Screw you loser..."

He's on his feet now. Big dude, Brett, the type who runs and lifts every day despite his crowded schedule, same as Decker. What he really needs to do is chill a bit, smoke a bit of weed, listen to some 'gaze, but don't think this is the time to tell him. Decker's just about restraining him and saying something I can't catch in his ear.

"Guys, tearing at each other's throats isn't getting us anywhere. We're all emotional. Let's just take a deep breathe, OK? Danny, looks like they're ready to take your order up there."

It's Sarah, our class social secretary, from my study group. Though I never really hung with her I always thought she was OK. Now she's probably just saved my ass. I put my hands up in a gesture of conciliation, turn and leave without my coffee. I look back on my way out the door and they're all staring at me. Figure that's those networking opportunities screwed. Guess they've kinda got a point though.

Go into the bank and get the cash, feel a bit paranoid walking out with two thousand pounds in my pocket. Not surprising after everything that's happened I guess. The wad of money feels good in my inside jacket pocket. Tempted for a moment to just take it, get in the car and drive up to Manchester, but that'd be a cop out. Instead, I call Harry and he agrees to meet me later, says he's got a few things to do when he gets back from the court. He'll call me when he's through. Go back home and spend pointless couple of hours trying to study. No way can I get my head around some academic bullshit about how corporations should adopt a strategy for worldwide competitive advantage. Tough gig at the best of times never mind now. Imagine spending three months of your life learning this stuff and then having nothing to show for it at the end? That happens to me and I'm gonna feel like slitting my wrists. Finally, Harry calls about two o'clock, we meet twenty minutes later round at his place. I give him the money, he doesn't count it.

"So, how's Balbeck then, he holding up OK?"

Harry shakes his head.

"Dunno. I mean, he seems weird but what else do you expect? Anyway, I don't really know the guy so it's difficult to say. Kept going on about shame and honour and stuff in the car. Then again, they're a pretty fatalistic bunch, these Russians."

"He's Kyrgyz actually, dude."

"Yeah, well, same thing really. I just hope the Dean goes easy on him. He should have been to see her by now."

"Let's call him."

"OK, you got his number?"

"No, you?"

"No, hang on there's a profile book here somewhere, should be in there."

Harry goes through a pile of papers and magazines on his table, don't think Balbeck's number's gonna be listed in FHM or Loaded somehow. Finally he produces it. We find the number. It's a landline, there's no mobile listed. Harry calls it.

"There's no answer. He can't still be with the Dean, we got back a couple of hours ago. She'll have wanted to see him straight away."

We look at each other. Shit we've posted ten grand of bail, what if the dude's absconded?

"Maybe we should go round there man, just check he's OK?"

"Good idea, we'll take my car, it's only ten minutes away."

Traffic's heavy and Harry's swearing and blaring his horn, neither of which gets us there any quicker. Neither of us are saying much on the way over either, but pretty certain Harry's hoping the same thing I'm hoping: Balbeck better be home. We get there, man this is pretty crummy accommodation. Mine ain't the Ritz but Balbeck's really flying coach class here. Mind you, his next accommodation

124

probably ain't gonna scrub up any better. We go up the communal stairs in the purpose built four storey block, the sort of soulless refuge that kinda sucks the spirit out of anyone living there. He's on the top floor. Harry knocks the door, no answer, then he knocks again harder.

"Maybe he's out?"

"Yeah, but where? There's no classes now and he's not exactly going to go out and party, is he?"

I shrug my shoulders, peer through the window into his tiny studio. It's dark in there. Hang on, it's OK, I can see him. At least those look like his legs behind the sofa, must be standing on something that I can't see properly.

"There he is, I think he's standing on a chair. Guess he's painting the ceiling or something."

"He's not painting the fucking ceiling. The stupid cunt's about to hang himself!"

Balbeck Toyevski

You have struggled for hours to tell Tamara how you feel. Explaining what has happened is the easy part. It is offering her a future that is difficult. You know she deserves more but still you do not want to let her go. Trying to tell her how you feel only sinks you deeper into despair. The words just will not come. You used to write poetry for your girlfriends before Tamara. Silly, childish stuff, comparing your love to mountains and oceans, but they liked it. You have never written a poem for Tamara. Nothing you could write would begin to describe your love for her. You can see her as you try to write, laughing in the sunshine. It is the day you were awarded the scholarship to study here. Her hair long and dark, her blue eyes sparkling as you tell her the news. You were out of breath because you had run so fast to find her after the professor spoke to you. He had wanted to keep you in his study, telling you of the great opportunity that had been secured for you. Making sure you knew of his role in your success. Reminding you to speak highly of the University here in Bishkek, when you were in England, to mention his name to your professors over there and how highly regarded his research was in the whole of Central Asia. But you were impatient of his self-serving chatter, needed to get out, to find Tamara. All the plans you made together that day: discussing what you would do when you came back home after the MBA, how there were so many new foreign companies looking to do business in central Asia, all keen to invest in your country and its people. Of course you

125

know that they are attracted by the gold and minerals Kyrgyzstan possesses, that will create opportunities for smart people like you to do business with them.

You stood holding hands in the sunshine making plans for Tamara and your brothers to come and visit you in England. She was breathless with excitement as she listed all the places she wanted to visit: Buckingham Palace, Big Ben, the Tower of London. You had to remind her that you were there to study, not be a tourist. But you smiled as you did so, secretly sharing her excitement at the thought of visiting these places together. How proud you felt when she phoned her father in Osh to tell him the news. He asked to speak with you himself to congratulate you. It was the first time he had spoken with you. You could hear the respect in his voice. He knew that you were worthy of his daughter, even though your family were not rich. For a moment, anger overcame your pride. Had he thought you a peasant? A low-life who would kidnap his daughter and then spoil her so no other man would want her? Treating her little better than a beast, only good for working and bearing children while you sat drinking and watching TV in a house with paint that stuck like gum to the walls? You were not brought up to believe that a man takes and a woman yields. But you could not stay angry with him. It is a father's duty to protect his daughter. In years to come you will do the same. But what will Tamara's father think of you now? Will her eyes ever sparkle again after what you have done? Now the only place she and your brothers can visit you is in prison.

The chair is just the right height to reach the ceiling. The legs are wobbly but that is OK. This will not take long.

Danny McMullen

Harry shoves me out of the way to look through the window, then starts to try to kick the door in. I join in. We're not heavy weights but the door gives way pretty easily and we spill in to the room.

"Balbeck it ain't worth it man, believe me. I've nearly been there myself but life goes on...."

We're lying on the floor where I managed to grab him and knock him off the chair. He looks stunned, he's shouting something in what must be Kyrgyz.

"Danny mate, there's no fucking rope here. What's happening then, Balbeck? Talk to us!"

126

"Why you kick in my door, assholes? Have you not caused me enough problems? Can you not leave me in peace, you motherfuckers?"

He's crying now. Looks angry too. Remember what happened with Rio and for a second I'm scared of him. I get up and look at Harry, he's right, there's no rope, or anything else. Only a broken light bulb.

"Balbeck, we're sorry man. We like thought you were, you know.."

"You thought what, tell me? Tell me why you kicked my door down and came in here like this."

"Mate, Danny and I, we thought, well, we thought you were going to hang yourself. I'm sorry, I know it sounds ridiculous…"

"Hang myself? Why? Because I have to go to jail? Because I will not be allowed to finish the MBA? Because of these things you think I would hang myself? You do not know anything about me, yet you believe I would take my life over such things. Are you fucking stupid?"

He's pissed at us. He's also right. Harry and I glance at each other.

"Listen mate, we only came over because we're concerned. We tried to call first but there was no answer."

"Concerned about me or concerned I would run away and you would lose your money, tell me?"

I look at the floor at this point, pretty certain Harry's doing likewise, but Balbeck's tone seems a bit softer.

"Listen, I did not answer the telephone because I had gone to the shops to buy a new light bulb. I was writing to my girlfriend, Tamara and my family, explaining everything that had happened. Telling them it might be years before I was back, that I hoped Tamara would wait for me, but I would understand if she didn't. Then the light bulb went off. I knew I needed a new one so I left to get it. When I came back I was changing over the bulb and then this happens. You guys turn up and kick my door in."

"Sure man, we understand totally. Look, we just came to see you were OK. Now we know you are, we'll like, just leave you to chill. Is that cool?"

"It is OK. I'm sorry I got so angry with you. I know you were only concerned for me. You are good friends."

"Obviously we'll pay for the damage to the door mate, that right Danny?"

"Of course dude, let us know how much it costs, or instead here's like twenty pounds. If we each give you that it should cover it."

"Fuck the door man, it was a piece of crap anyway. Like everything else in this fucking country. We have stronger doors in Kyrgyzstan and we do not even have anything worth stealing there."

Balbeck starts to laugh then Harry joins in. I ask them what's so funny, but I think I know, then I start laughing too.

Simone Sanders

Friday afternoon. Get back from my daily run. Sweated all those toxins out of my system over the past couple of days, back to feeling more like my old self again. Was on a bit of a comedown yesterday from all the coke and the anniversary of the abortion didn't help, but that's over with now. Need to be careful: was in danger of starting to let things slide a bit, can't afford to let that happen. Important to make up for lost time to-day, so sent out a dozen resumes, then hit the books for a few hours exam study. Had to bitch-slap some dumb-ass in the careers service earlier who hadn't followed up a lead I gave her. Client of mine whose started his own hedge fund over in London. No good to me as I'm back to the good old US of A once this is all over, but secure a few people here hedge fund interviews and favours are gonna be owed. I mean, I gave her the lead two days ago and she hasn't followed up on it yet. Think that's impressive? Few more things need to be taken care of now though. About time I let people know that Simone Sanders is back with the programme again. Take a shower, or rather the piss poor excuse for one in this country, then decide I'll send out an e-mail to the whole class clarifying my position on the events of recent days. I mean, it's no big deal, we all go a little wild and crazy sometimes, right? Takes me a while to compose it, need to strike the right tone here. Let them know that I acknowledge that by my own high standards I've been a bit behind the curve, but turn that to my advantage. Show I'm human after all. Need something suitably poetic and uplifting. Remember I've got a volume of American poetry on the bookcase, more for show than anything. Should get some inspiration there. Walt Whitman, perfect, that should do it. Send it and then call Sarah Jenkins, our class social rep. Can't stand the bitch to be truthful, but she does influence the social diaries of those who matter.

"Sarah, Simone. Hi sweetie, so tell me how are you? I just loved that dress you wore to the dinner. It was simply adorable. Yeah... oh of course it was a trouser suit, I'm a real dumb-ass sometimes, all this pressure they pile on you here. I just remember you looked to die for. You gotta give me the name of your hairdresser, I just can't find a local one, always end up having to go to London. Anyway, I wondered if you'd like to grab dinner, my treat. It's been a while since we had a proper talk...You have? Oh, ok, that's a drag, was hoping to catch up. No matter. Maybe tomorrow...Oh I see, sure don't blame you for heading out of this place for a few days. Glasgow sounds much more exciting. Well, you've got my cell so just call me anytime and we'll hook up. Of course, I've got a zillion things on myself, but you know, I can always make time for the special people like you."

Fucking hard-ass bitch, should be kissing my ass for the chance to hang around with me. Talk about not being there to support your colleagues in their hour of need. I won't forget this in a hurry. Where the fuck is Glasgow anyway, is that in Wales or something? Next try Hilary Jenkins-Spire but just get a snooty recording on her voice-mail informing me "as you can tell, I am currently unavailable, but please do not hesitate to leave a message which I shall endeavour to return as soon as possible". Whatever, these bitches better not be blanking me. Tabbing through the numbers on my cell when I come across Billy's. Shit for a second I'm tempted to call him see if he's still dealing. Fuck that's just dumb, he'll turn me straight over to the cops. I cross the room and sit down. For the first time I've realised I am gonna have to straighten out, get off this stuff. Never been a problem before but then I've never been using like I have since what happened with Patrick. I'm breathing heavily, wonder if I have just a little left, just to wean me off it? Won't take it now of course, save it for later. Well, maybe just enough to give myself a little lift, then I'll round up the other American girls. We can go bitch about the Brits. My black Donna Karen coat, must be some around somewhere, no. My leather jacket, no, jeans, no, no, no, fuck it my clothes are everywhere but I can't find what I need. What I've needed for a while now. Didn't used to. When Patrick got me started it was just fun. How else could we fuck all night and still pull our quotas on the phone in the morning? He'd come over to me at work with a glint in his eye.

"We're just being true professionals Simone, busting balls for the firm. Talking of which..."

Being naughty was thrilling. But Patrick's gone and the thrill with it. When he dumped me he felt it necessary to "express my concern over your habit". The lying two-faced gutless fuck.

I sit on the bed for the longest time, staring at Billy's number, but I don't call. I'm still sitting there when I hear a knock at the door. Better not be Harry still trying to sell me a sob story over

129

Balbeck. Like I haven't got enough crap of my own to deal with. Suppose I better get rid of whoever it is.

Shit, it's my mother.

Chapter Eleven

Danny McMullen

F azed me out a bit dude, and no mistake, that whole thing with Balbeck. For a minute there when I saw him lying on the floor with the chair kicked over, I really thought that was all she wrote. Reckon he's gonna get through it though. Harry's confident 'cause he's pleading guilty and everything he'll be out in a year or two. Apparently there's a possibility the business school will even let him finish the course then. He seemed OK when we left him. I think he just wants to be left alone. Let's face it, the rest of us are planning our glittering futures and he's about to do some hard time. Wouldn't exactly swap places with him, would you?

It's early evening now and I'm back at my room. Check on my e-mails, there's one here from Simone to the whole class:

"Dear Colleagues,
This term has been a transformational experience for me. I realise now that I arrived here with an overwhelming focus on external measures of success, how I was perceived by you all, rather than on my own personal fulfilment. I believed I could lead by excelling in everything I did. By showing, not telling, by setting the bar that little higher for myself every day. Along the way, I lost sight of what makes this whole experience so special, namely our interaction with each other. I lost sight of my responsibility to you all. For that I apologise and give you my assurance that from now on, I will be seeking to help you learn from my experiences, to help you deal with the profound transformation that this year is having on all our lives, to help you reach your own personal fulfilment. When I celebrate you, I celebrate myself.
Later,
Simone"

Shit man, "celebrate you I celebrate myself", didn't have Simone down for a'gaze fan. Just shows you never should judge.

Miguel calls, says he's got some new vinyl: Low, and God Speed You Black Emperor. Reckons it's the real deal. Says it's about time I broadened my horizons a bit, 1991 was a long time ago. Tell him to bring it over, we'll have a smoke and a listen. Nice mellow evening before I head up to Manchester tomorrow morning to see Caitlin. Think about trying to study but fuck that. Instead have a bath and listen to a bit of early Slowdive, back when they had their shit together enough to let Rachel Goswell do most of the singing. The sound of her voice mellows me out, just like it always has and always will, right from the first time I heard it all those years ago. Back when I was an undergrad in Canada, spending my days just smoking weed and listening to music. Course we were always looking for bragging rights from something new, before deciding it was outmoded soon as we found it. Then I heard "Avalyn". Sneaked the vinyl out of the party amongst the records I brought which all seemed so irrelevant suddenly. Sat up all night in my room listening to it. Played it the night Caitlin was born too, when they kept her and Karen in hospital overnight. Accompanied it with the best part of a bottle of Crown Royal. Should have felt tired and hungover the next morning and guess I was the last Dad to turn up in the post-natal ward, but carrying my daughter to our car I felt something unusual swelling up in me as I kissed her head: pride. Karen was bitching 'cause I'd forgotten to bring any more clothes, so Caitlin's first venture into the outside world was barefoot. I just held her tight and wrapped a blanket round her. Tomorrow I get to see her, get to hold her again. Even though the days since I carried her to the car have turned into years, my pride's never dimmed. Get to thinking that, ok, so maybe the other night ended in disaster, actually no maybe about it, but at least it reminded me I was still alive. Wonder if some lucky sonofabitch ended up going home with that sexy Belgian chick and her friend in the end? Maybe she did like me? Figure I can take a bit of confidence from something like that. I mean, Karen's long gone, Simone's a lost cause and I can't spend my whole life waiting for Rachel. Maybe I'll wait 'til Balbeck gets out of jail, go live in Kyrgyzstan for a while and hook up with one of those hot Peace Corp chicks he was talking about. Open a nightclub playing the 'gaze. Man, that would be awesome, talk about an alternative career path. Know I'll never do it because of Caitlin, but still it's positive thinking and that's what I need right now. Start doing what they tell us on this MBA - get out there and use my competitive advantage. Just need to work out what it is first. Am realising that's what this year's all about; acquiring a mindset, not some bullshit technical skills. Just as I start to skin up, Miguel calls back to say it's a fucking miserable evening, can I come and pick him up? Starts laying it on real thick. OK dude, I'll be there in half an hour.

132

So she's just standing there and I don't know what to say.

"Simone. Oh my darling. I'm so sorry."

Then she hugs me and we both start to cry, we stay like that for a long time. Finally, I bring her inside and we sit down.

"So what, how, I mean why are you here?"

"Your Dean called me yesterday in the middle of the night. She's a great lady, said she was worried about you, felt you were under a lot of strain. Asked me if you were coming home for Christmas. When I said you weren't she said she didn't think you should be left here all alone. So I got the next flight over. What's wrong, darling? I know you're not happy, and why are your clothes all over the floor?"

She's standing up now and looking distractedly round the apartment.

"Mom, sit down please. I'm OK, just a little stressed with all the workload. Honestly I'm fine, just trying to find something to wear. Meant to go out tonight, don't really want to but the girls on the course, they're just like so keen to hang out with me. Anyway, you didn't have to fly all the way over here. I mean, who's looking after Dad and what about your job? You can't just up and leave?"

"Your father will be fine, forget about us for a moment, you're what matters. It's always been that way for us. We both love you very much. You know that, don't you?"

"I guess so, I just want you to be proud of me. I've always felt guilty after what happened…"

She sits down again on the sofa, leaning forward and turning sideways to face me.

"Simone, Nicholas' death wasn't your fault, you were both children. It was a horrible accident."

"But it should have been me. I was supposed to be looking after him, he was my little brother. How can I not feel like it's my fault? After he died it just seemed like, I don't know, you guys gave up or something…"

She reaches out and takes my hand, which has been picking at the button of a cushion, then clasps it tightly and looks into my eyes, forcing me to meet her stare.

"Darling he chased his ball into the street, that's what kids do. Look at me Simone… you were so patient with him, playing ball for hours even though he was three years younger. What happened wasn't your fault, how could it have been? You were only seven years old. It wasn't anyone's fault, not even the kid who was driving the car. As for us giving up, Simone, we didn't. We just never started in the first place. We've always been content with what we have, because what we have is you."

"But that's never been enough for me, Mom. I'm sorry, I know that sounds so ungrateful."

"And that's OK, really it is. It's not being ungrateful to go out and stake your claim in life, to want more than we could give you, Simone. Just don't punish yourself for things that aren't your fault..."

She looks right at me the way she used to when I was a little girl and she was trying to tell me something important.

"... not even what happened when you were pregnant."

"But what...how did you know, I never told you..."

"Simone, I'm your Mother, you think I didn't know there was a reason why you moved back home, then came here? Why you weren't sleeping, all the pills you were taking? Eating next to nothing, exercising all the time, staying up in your bedroom and hardly talking to anyone? Think I didn't notice the way you threw yourself at that boy who worked at the gym? I may be old and poor and small-town and all those things you look down on, Simone, but I'm not stupid. Not where my own flesh and blood is concerned. I just wished you'd have let us help you, we so much wanted to. Your father never sleeps now, feels he's let you down, won't take any medication though. Says no way are they pumping his body full of chemicals. Stubborn sonofabitch, does he ever take a look at what he eats?"

We both start laughing. It feels cathartic.

"So why didn't you say something, Mom? I mean, if you knew about the...you know...and everything?"

"Simone, you're an adult now, you have been for a long time. You chose your own path in life and your father and I respect that."

Somehow, I don't know why, I feel the need to explain to her.

"The guy was married, that's why I couldn't have the baby. I loved him but he wouldn't leave his wife. I just couldn't face bringing up a child on my own. What it all meant. I didn't want the rest of my life to be spent as a struggle, just getting by, making do. Maybe I hoped if I had the abortion he wouldn't leave me. That things could go back to how they were before. How screwed up and selfish is that?"

I'm sobbing now and trying to say I'm sorry, she lifts my chin up.

"Don't be, it was your choice. You had to make it, no-one else, and you did. Don't for a second imagine that I think any less of you for it."

We hold hands without speaking, her grip's firm like it was when she said goodbye at the airport. This time though it's reassuring, not clasping. Suddenly, I realise how tired she must be...

"Mom, you must be exhausted. Do you need a shower or can I fix you something to eat? I don't have much in, but we can order in or go out."

"I'm fine sweetheart. Maybe I'll take a nap in a while, but I ate on the plane. You go ahead and fix yourself something if you're hungry though. You're too thin Simone, you're always too thin. I don't know where you got it from, certainly wasn't my side of the family."

I smile, it feels good to be here joshing with her.

"So how long you gonna stay, Mom? Guess Dad'll be wanting you home in a day or so?"

"You shouldn't be on your own for Christmas, Simone. If you won't come back to Iowa then I'll stay here, but we'd love you to come back. Your Dad has some plans for the store I know he'd like to run by you. He's been thinking of retiring and he's had some offers but you know how poor a head he's got for business, not like you. Guess you did get something from my side of the family after all."

"Well, I guess I could come back for a few days. I mean, I've got exams in January but I'm pretty much on top of things and it sounds like you guys need me back there."

"What about your evening with the girls?"

"Huh...oh that, it's OK. I'll tell them my Mom's in town. They'll understand."

"There's a flight tomorrow morning. We'll call your father later and tell him you'll be home for Christmas."

She picks up the photograph of the four of us on the mantelpiece that she pressed into my hands at the airport. We both stand and look at Nicholas smiling out at us before she hugs me for the second time that day. I don't let go.

Chapter Twelve

Harry Stanton

So I get back after dropping Danny off and there's a telephone message from the Dean. Informs me that after considerable deliberation at their board meeting this morning the business school have decided against taking any further action at present against Simone, Danny or I. Sweet. Any luck, that's the end of this little saga as far as I'm concerned. Feeling pretty knackered so reckon I'll have a quick kip then maybe head back down to London. Better phone round a few people and see what's going on, bound to be something on a Friday in Mid-December. No-one's answering, so leave a couple of messages then have a quick flick through the FT. Need to keep some handle on what's happening in the market. Phone goes, assume it's one of the lads calling me back about coming down tonight, so answer it without checking the name display. Big mistake: it's Theresa.

"Harry, it's Theresa. Why haven't you been returning my calls? What's wrong, don't you want to see me any more?"

Theresa, shit I'd almost forgotten about her. It's been a couple of weeks since our last little afternoon tryst. Bit bored with it to be honest. Nice enough girl, but she's only a kid, got fuck all in common and there's always another shagging opportunity around the corner. Although, probably not for a few weeks given the state of my face. With this in mind I'm tempted to get her over here, but sounds like she's about to go into one and fuck it, I don't need the aggro.

"Been busy sweetheart, this MBA's not like your little History course, five hours a week of classes or whatever. They work our asses off on this thing."

"Harry I know, I'm sorry. It's just that I miss you so much, angel."

Fuck it, I hate it when she calls me that. Even more so when she does so in that needy voice like she's vested all her hopes for future happiness in me. Bad move if she has.

"Why don't we get together tonight? Come over and we can be together before I go home for the holidays tomorrow."

"Sorry sweetheart, no can do. I've made arrangements to go down to London."

"But that means I won't see you for a whole month. Unless you'll come and visit me at my parents?"

No fucking chance.

"That's going to be very difficult I'm afraid. To be honest, I don't really have the time to see anyone right now. Got exams coming up and all that, you know how it is. Best you just go on home for the holidays. We'll see how things are in the new year."

"What do you mean, see how things are in the new year? Harry, what are you trying to say here? Please tell me you're not dumping me?"

"Look, it's not that I don't want to be with you. It's just, well…to be honest I just don't have the time for a relationship right now."

"But I thought you loved me? Harry, you said that…"

Her voice is breaking up when she says this. Can picture the tears starting to flow. She's not the first I've reduced to tears and she won't be the last. Don't set out to do it, just don't want to deal with this shit when it gets heavy. As for do I love her? Truth is I don't even know the girl. Never give her more than a passing moment's thought unless we were in bed together, and even then it was just you know…casual.

"Theresa, you're a sweet kid. You'll find someone right for you, someone your own age. We've had a bit of fun. Let's just leave it at that, ok?"

Then I mutter something about having to go and put the phone down on her as she breaks out sobbing. Not proud of myself, but fuck it, I never made any promises. This has been a pretty shit couple of days. Fuck it, I'm getting cleaned up and down to London. Why the fuck hasn't anyone called me back? Swear to God, you take a year out and it's like every fucker forgets about you. That's one thing they neglect to mention in the brochures.

Lying in the bath, looking at Marianna in the bikini photo I managed to steal from her room. She's standing on a beach with one of her feet raised on a sunbed letting me see all the way up the inside of her thigh. There's a glass of red wine in her hand that's nearly empty and the sun's setting behind her. You just know that within a few hours she'll be naked with Carlos' cock inside her. It's only a snapshot, no doubt taken by a shirtless Carlos who appears in most of the other photos, but every time I look at it, it feels like I'm seeing it for the first time. Things are building nicely when interrupted by someone ringing my buzzer constantly. Think about ignoring it, but the moment has passed. Bet it's Theresa come round to try and make up, fucked if I want to deal with that right now. Mind you, if she has came all the way over here it'd be rude to show her the door straight away. Wrap the towel round me and

138

go to answer it but when I do there's no one there, strange. Little disappointed for a minute but Marianna's photo compensates more than satisfactorily. Finally, I get a text message, everyone's meeting up later in Smithfield market. Fine, I'll be there. Decide to get changed and get out of here. I'll grab something to eat in London. Think I'll stay down there 'til the start of the new term. Had enough of this place for a while. Need to do a bit of networking as well, find out who might be hiring in the summer when this thing's over. Don't want to find myself renting some booth in a prop trading outfit after all this. Market's picked up nicely though so should be OK. Reckon the long only game's a bit tired, maybe try and use this MBA to get into private equity. Seems that's where the real action is now and some of the stuff we learn on here might just be useful for that too. I'll have a chat with a few people tonight, find out what's what. Get outside where it's fucking dark now and cold, rain's coming down in diagonal slants and carving into my face. For a minute I'm tempted to just fuck off back inside, order a pizza and put my feet up. Maybe call big Sean and get him over for a couple of cans and a session on the Playstation but bugger it, I need some civilization. Gets to you sometimes, this business school shit. Run across to the car park at the back of the building. Pretty deserted. Least I've got remote controlled locking so jump straight in the car. Fumble round in the back, there should be a towel in there somewhere. Someone opens the passenger car door. I've fucking told Theresa it's over...

"Allright Harry. Nice motor."

What the fuck? Turn round and there's a gun barrel pushed up against my nose, forcing my head back.

"OK...OK...just...just take it easy."

I put my hands up by my sides at shoulder height. I'm looking down but I can't see the bloke's face. He's got a ski mask on. He lowers the gun into my ribs and tells me to drive to the river, now.

"I ain't telling you this again, Harry, and I ain't fuckin' around. Try anything funny and your brains are all over the fuckin' windscreen, understand?"

"Whatever you say, mate. Just don't do anything stupid. We can try and sort this out, whatever it is."

"It's well late for that, just drive."

"OK, sure, not a problem."

He takes off the mask as I start the car up and pull out of the car park, but pulls the hood of his fleece down half-way over his forehead, and his zipper up to cover his mouth. He's saying nothing other than grunting directions. We're headed towards the river, traffic's light and visibility's crap. No way is anyone going to realise anything's up here. With his free hand he holds a cigarette packet up to his mouth, puts a cigarette in his mouth and takes one out. Then lights it. Doesn't offer me one.

"What do you want with me? Look, if it's money we can sort something."

"My brother's dead 'cause of you. Your money gonna bring him back is it?"

So that's what this is all about then. There's a catch in his voice when he says this. Need to play for time here, that's all I can think of right now.

"You mean Rio? Look that was an accident, we're all really upset about it."

"'Course you're upset, bet you were all going to come to the funeral next Tuesday, weren't you? Maybe have a collection for his son and girlfriend, eh? That right Harry, you rich cunts all broke up about killing my brother then?"

He's breathing heavily now and the gun's jamming harder into my nozzle. He tells me to turn in on the right up ahead. Recognise where we are now, that's where we dumped Simone's stuff that afternoon. Fuck, that seems like a lifetime ago.

"Like I said, if it's money you want then just tell me. I'll see his family OK, can't do that if I'm dead though."

Fuck! He punches me hard in the mouth, my lip starts to bleed.

"I'll decide what you can and can't do! Right, you fucking got that?"

He punches me again. I spit out some blood but I make it seem worse than it really is. I manage to get a bit of a look at him, realise this guy's a bit younger and smaller than Rio. His eyes look pretty glazed though and I reckon he's just about keeping it together. He loses it and I could be dead. Not like this. Christ, I've barely turned thirty.

I hear the sound of a screw cap being opened and smell cheap whiskey. The booze sloshes around in the bottle after he's swilled it back.

"Just don't piss me about Harry. It's this fucking turn up here on the right."

He's slurring his words now. He takes another swallow then throws what sounds like an empty bottle into the back seat. Must have been drinking before turning up at my place. Guess it's to give him the courage to shoot me. Check my rear-view mirror: there's a small car with a woman driving and child up front, fuck it, slow down to let them pass on the outer lane. Come on, come on, you stupid bitch, this turning's almost upon us. Finally, she crawls past.

140

What's behind now? A VW Golf with a single driver. It's a couple of years old judging by the number plate, but it'll still have an air-bag. This'll have to do. I sink the accelerator to the floor, put some distance between me and the VW, then slam on the brakes and swing the car hard left. The VW ploughs into the passenger side. My car does a 90 degree spin leaving me face on with the driver of the Golf. Danny fucking McMullen.

Danny McMullen

I'm in the car driving over to Miguel's, got Mogwai playing on the CD. Good driving music man, keeps the vibe going. Tight-ass bastard Miguel coulda taken a taxi I guess, but no big deal. It ain't far to his place, and it is a shitty evening. Fucking rain's coming down so hard I can't see shit. I hope it's not like this for the drive to Manchester tomorrow. I like the drive up there, gives me a chance to listen to some sounds for a few hours, uninterrupted. Usually mix it up a bit, play some newer stuff when I set out, then the classics as I get closer to Manchester and Caitlin. Need something familiar that'll reassure me she's still gonna smile when she sees me. Do the reverse on the way back. Always need a lift when I say goodbye to my daughter. Help block out the tears I've just heard her shed. Not a good time for experimenting. Better not get too fucked up tonight just in case the weather stays like this. No way am I letting Caitlin down. Jesus Christ! Slam on the brakes but it's too late...

I'm feeling kinda groggy but think I'm still alive, then I hear a familiar voice trying to make itself heard over Mogwai performing one of their customary gear changes from quiet to loud...

"Danny mate, you OK? Listen, just get the fuck out of the car. Rio's brother's trying to shoot me. I'm fucking serious here Danny, that's why I had to crash into you."

I stagger out of the car, the airbag saved my life but what the fuck's going on here? What's Harry talking about?

"Harry, shit, what the fuck have you got a gun in your hand for?"

Other people have stopped, some chick's talking to us now, telling us she's called an ambulance. Harry's shoved the gun in his pocket, then a young guy staggers out of Harry's car and is tumbling down the grass verge towards the river. Harry leaves me and pushes through people to run after him. I get up and stagger after Harry. The guy runs to the pier where we dumped Simone's stuff from. Harry follows him until he gets to the end of it. I join them. I'm bent over double 'cause I'm fucking winded. Harry's talking to the guy now.

"So you were going to shoot me then, that right mate?"

"No mate, I swear to you, please. I was just trying to scare you a bit, get some cash out of you, for Rio's family like. I wouldn't have shot you mate, no way, swear on me mother's life."

Harry points the gun at him.

"Harry man, don't shoot him. You'll never be able to live with yourself. The police are coming - we'll just let them deal with it."

"Why shouldn't I shoot him, Danny? He was threatening to shoot me, maybe come after you next, ever think of that?"

"He's just a kid Harry. He's lost his brother. Like he says, he wasn't trying to shoot you."

In the background I hear a siren, either ambulance or police. Fuck, I'll be glad when someone gets here, this is a weird gig and getting weirder. I keep pleading with Harry but he's ignoring me now and pointing the gun at this guy. The dude's sobbing now, keeps muttering that he wasn't going to shoot anyone. Says he's got to look after his brother's family now Rio's dead. That he was just gonna take Harry's car and then leave him here. Sounds like he's telling the truth, too. Fuck, he's young. Can't be more than about eighteen. Harry's hand's steady on the gun, and he's keeping it pushed into this kid's face.

"Not very pleasant is it, having a fucking gun pointed in your face, eh?"

Now the kid's shaking his head and grunting something unintelligible. Shit, I'm gonna have to try and jump Harry and get the gun off him. I'm a good twenty pounds heavier but there's a look of being in control in Harry's eyes that makes me hesitate. Then he pulls the trigger.

Harry Stanton

'Course first thing I did when I crashed was to grab the gun. Wasn't difficult as this guy's head smacked hard against the side windscreen, almost knocking him out. Then I was out of the car. Checked Danny was OK, then saw this wanker was trying to leg it. No fucking chance pal, need to play this so I'm not looking over my shoulder the rest of my life. Chased him down the verge and caught up with him on the peer, now it's time to make sure this is over. Thought this might just be a replica gun, but from the way he's quivering and jibbering when I point it at him it must be the real thing. Good. He drops to his knees into a puddle of water

142

whimpering that he's sorry. I lower the gun and pull the trigger. The empty chamber clicks. I look at him. He's still wide-eyed with fear. Smells like he's shat himself as well.

"I'm not a killer, neither are you, and neither's our friend who kicked your brother in front of the police van. I'm sorry about your brother, we all are, but it was a fucking accident. Now this gun's got your prints all over it and I'm keeping it. So fuck off out of here and I don't ever want to see you again. You understand what I'm telling you?"

He's nodding as he legs it off the pier, stopping to throw up on the way.

"You're not telling the cops?"

"No Danny, I'm not. Any idea how much hassle it'd be for all of us? You and I go back up there and tell everyone I skidded and crashed. Our friend here was never in the car, no-one's going to remember seeing him and even if they do, so what? A night like tonight, people just want to get back in their cars and fuck off home."

"Think he'll try anything again?"

"I doubt it. I could've handed him over to the police and I didn't. He knows it's over. Don't think he'd have gone through with killing me anyway, but couldn't risk it. Let's get up there and see if our cars are still driveable."

On the way up the verge, Danny asks me how I knew the gun was empty.

"I took the bullets out when I was chasing him, just wanted to scare him a bit. No way was I getting caught with a loaded gun by the police."

He smiles at me and shakes his head. Then we get back to the cars and tell the ambulance crew we're both fine, just a bit shaken. No-one else has been caught up in the accident. The police turn up and act pretty disinterested. Once they determine we're both sober they just take a brief statement and go. Both cars are smashed up pretty good but still look driveable. Danny's is damaged a shed-load more than mine, story of his life I guess.

"Sorry about your car. Reckon it'll be OK to get you home though. Do you need me to follow you just in case?"

"Thanks, but it's tomorrow I'm bummed about. Was meant to be driving to Manchester to visit my daughter. No way this thing's gonna get me up there now. Guess I'll have to take the train."

"Didn't know you had a daughter, mate. Can't be easy if she's all the way up there?"

He just shrugs, then brings out his wallet and shows me a picture of a little girl in a blue dress.

"She's beautiful, must take after her Mum. You guys not together any more then?"

He looks awkward and just shrugs.

Tell him I'm sorry but he must be proud of his daughter.

"Yeah, I am. She's what keeps me going. That and the music. Remember when I tried to ask you about it at the beginning of term?"

Actually look at the guy properly for the first time, covered in mud from where he must have fallen coming down the verge. They weren't kidding when they said the MBA threw people from different backgrounds together into pressurised situations. Doubt if what we've been through in the first term was quite what they had in mind though. Christ knows what the rest of the year's gonna be like, just fucking glad I didn't sign up for a two year programme.

"What, that first night at the beginning of term when we were having a few drinks in the pub?"

"Yeah. Surprised you even remember."

"Just there's something I've been meaning to ask you since."

"Let me guess Harry, you want to know what a loser like me's doing here, right?"

"No, sod that mate. You're here for the same reason as the rest of us. To fill the gaps in our empty little lives. Nope, what I really want to know is… just what the fuck is shoegazing anyway?"

Epilogue

Poor Balbeck. I need you to listen to me now, my handsome and clever son. How I wish I could take your head in my hands and look into your eyes when I tell you this. For so many long hard years you've carried the burden of being the eldest, the man of the house. It is because of you that Mother's back is still straight, her hands still soft. Your example has helped your younger brothers become men with dreams of a world outside Bishkek. They walk with their heads held high on the soil under which I am buried. When you were eight years old, the last thing I told you was how I would always be looking over you. I will keep my promise, do not doubt me now. Your brothers will look after mother, it is their turn now. Do not feel you have let people down, no father could be prouder of his son than I am of you. Be strong and remember who you are. Have you not been through worse than this? When you get out of prison you can leave this country and go home, back to where you belong. The lawyer says you will be home in eighteen months. It will be summertime in the Tien Shan mountains and Lake Ysyk-kul will be at its most beautiful. Tamara will be waiting there for you. For you my son, it will be blue skied 'n' clear.

Printed in the United Kingdom
by Lightning Source UK Ltd.
117040UKS00001B/292-306

9 781904 433644